HARTFORDS

Katherine Spearing

♡ *Katherine*

ISBN Ebook: 9781736711910
ISBN Paperback: 9781736711903

This is a work of fiction. All names, characters, places,
and occurrences are either a product of the authors
imagination or are used fictitiously. Any resemblance to
actual persons, businesses, events, or locations is entirely
coincidental. The publisher does not have any control over
and does not assume any responsibility for the author or
third-party websites or their content.

Dedicated to my four sisters.
(Obviously)

Contents

AUTHOR'S NOTE

I was one of five sisters, and while it might seem an easy thing to base the story of the Hartford sisters around my own experience, my upbringing was quite the opposite.

While the Hartfords are attracting stares and gossip because they are defying convention by crafting lives that weren't defined by husbands, I grew up in a world trying to turn back time, giving very defined gender roles to men and women.

Women were to cook, clean, and sew. Men were sent out into the world to slay dragons and bring home a paycheck. We were never told women could do anything men could do. While the Hartfords were raised not to depend upon marriage, we believed marriage was our only hope.

More than most, I resonated with books like *Little Women* or *Pride and Prejudice*. I truly understood what it was like to have a whole world of possibilities denied because of gender. I understood what it was like to feel your whole life depended upon marrying well.

So here, I did a bit of an experiment. I took a time period (1840s New England) where women were resigned to homemaking and men were resigned to bread-winning and asked the question, what if a whole family decided all that convention was ridiculous?

Still, the story centers around matchmaking and finding husbands. When people fall in love, they get married. The main difference is the friendships between the men and women, and how they find allies in one another.

Unashamedly, I took all my favorite things from Austen, Alcott, and the Brontës, put them in a salad, and made a pizza.

I hope you enjoy my Hartford sisters.

1

The Hartford Family's Greatest Critic

Some said the Hartford sisters would never marry, but not for reasons the general populace might suppose. They were not ugly, by any means. In actuality, they were quite handsome. They were not dull. To be sure, they were widely known for their vitality and jolly dispositions. What then, you may wonder, is the reason behind this presumed fate of spinsterhood that the Hartford sisters were altogether doomed to?

An unmarried woman was considered a blight on society, though it was not uncommon for one, or even two daughters for that matter, to not be given in matrimony. Nevertheless, it would make the Hartford sisters' case unusual, if none of them ever married. For there were five of them: Samantha, Rose, Allison, Elizabeth, and Victoria. All close in age, all close in relationship. But we will address their individualities later. For now, we are discussing the reason behind the assumption they would never marry.

Men are not driven away by good looks or

appealing personalities. If they were, perhaps these unchangeables might make the Hartfords' destiny a little easier to bear (as these traits are not acquired by choice). The answer to the question is deliberate unconventionality.

The world of Tree Town—and the world at large—was a conventional, well-regulated ship that sliced through the waters of progress with orderliness and decorum. There were rules for the upper class and rules for the lower class and rules for men and rules for women.

The Hartfords followed none of these rules.

By virtue of their financial situation, they might have been considered upper-class, as the father was a successful and respected merchant and estate owner. They did not acquire their wealth in the usual way (through inheritance), but in the age of progress, that was becoming less important. They were quite wealthy, yet the daughters did not behave as other wealthy daughters. They did not merely sit around at the pianoforte or learn the latest dances or sew dresses for fine parties at the coast.

Rather, they worked alongside the working men of the field. They attended business negotiations with their father.

And they read books.

Ghastly, it was considered. It was rumored once at a gathering in Port Town that Allison, the third-born, crossed the drawing room to join a group of men in their discussion of farming stocks.

The men were quite uncomfortable with a young woman knowing so much about money and exchange. With such feminine duties neglected and such masculine duties performed, it is no wonder their behavior would make them less attractive in the eyes of potential suitors.

For what man wishes a wife to be his equal in form and intellect?

You see their sorrow. You might have heard it whispered in town, *but they are such pretty girls,* as the waste of female suppleness disappeared before the eyes of the neighborhood. The future stretched out before the Hartford sisters in one long and solitary road of censure.

With this in mind, let us begin the story.

Along the cobble-stoned main street of Tree Town, a certain young gentleman named Daniel Copeland strolled. He was on his way to see with his own eyes the spectacle causing the greatest uproar since—well—he couldn't remember when. The rumor of this spectacle had reached his mother just the day before. She'd heard from a servant (who'd heard from Alma Burros) that the eldest Hartford sister had gotten married.

At first he was shocked (as everyone was) but he hid his shock behind a sardonic smile, saying to himself, "Well, some people do have an occasional stroke of luck."

He'd waited an entire day before tromping into town to see what everyone was talking about, allowing himself just a bit of curiosity.

What sort of man would marry a *Hartford?*

He forced himself to lag as he whistled absently. He was sure he would find the couple exactly as he'd been told: happy, in love, and extremely married.

He was nearly to the address of the newlyweds when he sucked in his breath and dodged into a shadow as two people came out the front door of his destination.

Alma Burros and Loretta Humphrey.

Alma Burros was a short plump woman with a plethora of gray hair piled on top of her head. She talked so fast sometimes, Daniel often wondered if she ever actually took a breath (or just had an extra store of it hidden somewhere). She had an uncanny ability of never letting you leave if she caught you long enough to begin a conversation.

He was in town to see the married Hartford. Not Alma Burros.

He did not like Alma Burros.

Loretta Humphrey was not so bad. She was moderately sensible (for a middle-aged woman) and didn't smile too much and mostly kept her opinion to herself. Her only flaw was her proximity to the Hartfords, as she was their neighbor.

And Daniel did not like the Hartfords.

A great deal could be said here about Daniel Copeland: He was the only son of a wealthy landowner (a member of the old aristocracy and patron of Tree Town). His widowed mother, Agnes Copeland, raised him. Though the woman did the best she could, raising a son without the aid of a husband was not a subject they had taught her in finishing school.

Tree Town had few children who were not of "the working class" and therefore very few children were suitable playmates for Daniel. Due to the business success of the Hartfords, Agnes Copeland deemed the sisters acceptable companions—for a time. Then they grew older, and she began to see them as independent, outspoken, and headstrong.

This was around the time Daniel began to adopt the characteristics of snobbery and selfishness not uncommon to members of the dwindling aristocracy. Alas, he was left to his own devices and kept mostly to himself.

Daniel hugged the wall of the building next to Samantha (formerly Hartford's) residence, waiting until Alma Burros and Loretta Humphrey had disappeared down Main Street. Once it was safe, he approached the townhome and rapped soundly on the front door. The queen of the household, Samantha, that is, opened it, and her blue eyes widened in surprise. "Daniel Copeland, you are the last person I expected to visit us during our first week in town." She smiled charmingly, and Daniel recollected he had always carried a small admiration for the eldest Hartford sister. She may now be a wife, but that admiration was untainted—though it remained just as small.

Daniel stepped into the foyer (noticing instantly how tight the entryway was) and with a bow and a wave of his hand said, "I have come to gawk, as everyone else has come to gawk. I am entitled to my share. Would you not agree?"

Samantha only laughed with fond pleasure and invited him into the parlor (which was also half the dining room). Daniel noted the size of the place was quite a step down from the accommodations Samantha had been accustomed to and wondered if this new husband was not quite as wealthy as everyone presumed.

He found himself in the company of three other persons. Mr. Sommers, the landlord, had come to inquire how the couple found the house. He brought along his wife, Mrs. Sommers. The third was a ruggedly handsome young man with light brown hair and a bit of a shadow of whiskers. He rose when Daniel entered, and Samantha moved to his side.

"This is William Temple," she said. (Was there a hint of pride in her voice?) The young man extended his hand to Daniel and gave him a well-bred "How do you do?"

Daniel was invited to take tea along with the other guests (though they were having tea for the third time that day). Mr. Sommers was in the middle of relating the details of an ocean voyage he had once endured, thus giving Daniel time to observe Tree Town's newest installment. He eyed William with censure, recognizing the man as someone he had seen around town once or twice in the recent months. He had heard from his mother (who had heard it from a servant who had heard it from Alma Burros) that William Temple was on business and was merely passing through. Daniel told himself later that he'd have to pay more attention from now on.

After Mr. Sommers had finished his story, they took their leave. Daniel found himself alone with William and Samantha.

The new lovers asked politely after the news of Tree

Town. Daniel was an astute student of Tree Town gossip, but assumed they had already heard the news ten times over. He preferred to steer the conversation in a different direction.

"I am curious to know," said Daniel. "How it came about that any Hartford daughter, or Hartford father, could shed their defenses long enough for a scalawag to actually marry you."

William turned to Samantha. "Did he just call me a scalawag?" he asked.

"Don't let his comments trouble you, love," said Samantha. "You see, Daniel is the Hartford family's greatest critic." She turned back to Daniel. "It's a rather short story, with the most interesting part being the elopement—that is to say—it was an elopement from the town, but not from my family. My family was present, as was William's. Both parents gave their blessing to the marriage. Our parents had become friends and introduced us in Port Town about six months ago. It was rather witty. Even they didn't think we would actually fall in love."

Daniel remembered a time when the Hartfords had gone to the coast during a particularly brutal New England October. He would never have guessed they were going to find a husband. He would have to watch their comings and goings more closely from now on.

"We had been corresponding for a few months," Samantha continued her tale. "When William came to our home and asked for my hand. We planned the wedding that same week. And now we are married." Samantha sighed and leaned back against her husband in a way that suggested she was pleased to finally be settled.

Daniel Copeland stroked his whiskers and surveyed the couple in their daze of contentment. Although he desired to bestow his blessing upon Samantha and her new husband, his habitual character prohibited it. As everyone in the town was displaying happiness for the couple, he felt it his duty to bring Samantha's joy to a steady, harsh reality. He did so by saying: "Quite a work of fate, you might say. Tis a pity, really, though I am happy for you both. I never could have imagined a Hartford stooping to the common pursuit of marriage. But as it is so, I am glad you were lucky enough to find happiness."

William's pleasant face suddenly became cold. He stiffened. Had it not been for Samantha's presence, he might have pounced on this one rain cloud that had dared to impinge upon his sunny world.

Samantha, however, was accustomed to Daniel and had never allowed his sour disposition to cause her grief. She often sought ways to lift him from his sullen moods and encourage him toward a more contented manner. But sometimes, she met him where he stood. Proving him wrong was a more beneficial course of action. So she challenged him: "Daniel, do you mean to say that I only married because I was lucky?"

"That I do," he replied.

"And that choice and desire had nothing to do with my happiness or my marriage?"

The question stumped Daniel. Though he believed Samantha to be a level-headed girl, he wanted to believe (along with the rest of the town) that their strange ways would not lead to success. He was also unhappy and, as previously mentioned, he was selfish. Unhappy, selfish people find it quite difficult when surrounded by the happiness of others.

Despite his unhappiness and his selfishness, Daniel would never wish to truly offend Samantha, and for a moment regretted ever saying a word to the contrary. That regret was fleeting, and his cynicism once again was his loyal friend.

"Samantha, you must have noticed your situation was long in coming." (She was twenty-four years old, after all.) "Considering this, your sisters will have a hard time of it. You may have procured a man worthy of your—devotion—" (What he wanted to say, was "a man strange enough to be interested in such an intelligent and outspoken woman.") "But such a man is rare." He leaned forward and with a flare of his hands said, "These rare men must reside in the remotest parts of the world. One of them may exist, but the chance that others exist—four to be precise— is unlikely. I mean only to say that I congratulate you, and I sincerely hope that I will someday be able to congratulate your sisters in the same way. But even you must admit that is highly unlikely."

Samantha merely smiled indulgently. "I don't know that it's unlikely at all."

"If you're so confident luck had nothing to do with it, then I wonder your other sisters are not more active in the marriage market."

"Whatever do you mean?"

It only took half a second, but something very wicked and entertaining burst into Daniel's mind. He grinned and sat up a bit straighter in his chair. "What do you say to a bit of wager?"

Samantha blinked. "Wort sort of wager?"

Daniel rubbed his hands together. "If your sisters are married by the end of the year, I promise to never say another word about 'luck' again."

"That's hardly fair."

"Fine then. Engaged. They have to be engaged by New Year's Eve."

Samantha's eyes narrowed, but her lips were relaxed in a smile. "And what might we get out of this? What happens if we win?"

Daniel chuckled. This was going to be very entertaining. It was impossible for any four sisters to secure proposals in one year and that would mean any ordinary sisters. The Hartfords were not like other girls and he knew for a fact they had received very few proposals.

The third born, Allison, had received exactly none.

No, they were all going to be spinsters and this bet was already won.

But, if Samantha excepted, her reward must be worth the price she had to pay (for her work was certainly cut out for her). "I'll never say an ill word about your family again—a gag for myself and all my decedents." Daniel gestured magnanimously.

Samantha tilted her head to the side, shaking it slightly.

"Fine, I'll apologize for all the ill words I've said in the past."

Samantha clasped her hands, waiting.

Daniel fumbled around in his brain. He could offer

to pay for the weddings, but the Lord knew the Hartfords didn't need the money. His horse? No, that wasn't suitable.

Samantha's eyes lit up. "I know," she said. "You must give a toast. A toast at each of their weddings, praising them and blessing their marriage. And each toast must be approved by us." She reached for William's hand.

William's eyes were wide with bewilderment and Daniel thought smugly that the new husband was just beginning to understand what sort of woman he'd married.

"You have a deal," said Daniel. "But what do I get if I win?" (He almost emphasized how likely this was, but decided better of it. Best not to scare the mouse in the trap.)

"It's hardly fair you'd win anything for doing nothing."

"True, true. But there's got to be stakes. Otherwise, you'll just give up if it becomes too difficult."

"I never back down from a challenge."

"No, I don't believe you would. But I want my winnings just the same."

"Very well, what is it you want?" Samantha pressed her lips together and waited patiently.

Daniel was elated. This was the most fun he'd had all day. All week for that matter. It might even be the most fun he'd had all year. "Something along the same lines," he decided. "An article in the The Post, singing my praises. And it must be approved by me." He flashed a mischievous grin. The townspeople would think the end of the world had arrived when they saw that article in the town paper with Samantha's byline.

There was a moment of deliberate silence, where the only sound was the ticking clock on the mantel. Samantha stared at Daniel, and he stared back, daring her to renege.

Samantha stood. She extended her hand. "Daniel Copeland, you have yourself a wager."

After briefly outlining the rules for the wager, Daniel left the couple and went in search of his next amusement.

After William had seen Daniel to the door, he returned to the parlor. He raised his eyebrows at his pretty wife and asked the question we are all asking at this moment: "What on earth were you thinking, Samantha?"

Samantha looked at him in bewilderment. "I have absolutely no idea."

William sank into the armchair as he said, "What have you gotten us into?" He folded his hands and for a while, both he and Samantha sat a moment staring wide-eyed at the tea table.

Samantha's face was downcast when she said, "I am going to take back the challenge. I will do it first thing in the morning. Though Daniel's darts and barbs will be worse afterward."

"No," said William. He was pensive and serious. "Something Daniel said gave me an idea. He said 'the remotest parts of the world.' When he said that, I thought of something. Men worthy of your sisters are rare. Perhaps they do lie in the remotest parts of the earth. If this is so, we must bring those men to your sisters." William's eyes were alight with a plan.

It was Samantha's turn to be perplexed. "How do you propose we do that?" she asked.

"I have a friend. His name is Reuben Dudley. He was my best chum from university and I had plans of hiring him to do some book-keeping for the shipping yard as soon as I am established. Perhaps we could extend him an invitation to visit and see how he likes Tree Town and the coast. Perhaps, just perhaps, he might form an attachment with one of your sisters. I am sure your family will love him."

Samantha's eyes glistened. William could have laughed or been angry at her agreement with Daniel, but instead he found it interesting and was now attempting to help her.

William looked at her earnestly. "I would never tamper with your sisters' hearts. We will bring Reuben here, but he must fall in love with one of them without any aid from us. Only, Daniel will know we are up to something if a stranger suddenly shows up in town—invited by us."

Samantha smiled. "Let him know. He's so confident we will lose, I doubt he'd try and sabotage." She reached for her husband's hand and pulled him over to the sofa beside her. She took his face in her hands and planted a kiss on his lips, her happiness enhanced by the thought one of her sisters might find themselves equally so in just a few short weeks.

2

I Don't Read Romances

Only a few days after the fateful day in which Daniel and Samantha struck a deal, the four sisters still bearing the name of Hartford paid a visit to their beloved older sister. With arms linked, Rose, Allison, Elizabeth, and Victoria cantered down Main Street in quest of the home of Samantha.

Samantha was expecting them, waiting with the door open as they approached.

Victoria, the youngest, broke free from the sisterly chain and ran into Samantha's arms. Elizabeth followed immediately behind Victoria. There was quite a scene of laughter, turning many an austere head from the other patrons of Main Street.

Conscious they were drawing attention, Allison and Rose waited to display their affection for their sister until they were safely inside.

Samantha had tea waiting. It seemed the little house could not contain the ecstasy of five sisters reunited. It exploded with their laughter as they all began speaking at once.

"How is the newest wife in Tree Town?" asked Allison, after she, Rose, and Elizabeth had squeezed together on the sofa.

"Perfectly well," said Samantha. "I love every minute of being married, I only wish my four sisters could be as happy." Though she and William had determined they could force none of the sisters to fall in love, Samantha considered herself a gardener. As such, she would plant as many seeds as she liked.

"If what they say of the Hartfords is true," said Allison. "None of us will ever marry."

"Samantha got married," said Elizabeth. "Why should the rest of us not share the same fate?"

"You will have no trouble, I'm sure," said Allison, poking Elizabeth in the ribs. She squealed in a very undignified way before whacking Allison on the arm.

"Don't let your suitors see you do that!" Allison crowed.

"Both of you, stop it," said Rose. "We are in our married sister's home. Have some respect."

But Samantha was laughing, arm draped around Victoria, who was suppressing giggles.

Allison relaxed back on the sofa. It had been more difficult for her than for the other sisters when the wings of love whisked Samantha away, but she concealed it behind quips and jests. Samantha had been her confidant for all of her grand plans, and once they were separated by marriage, she felt the lonely hole deep within her chest.

Allison had dark hair and sun-tanned skin, though it was far from fashionable, and gave her away as a working girl the moment anyone saw her. She enjoyed working out of doors and frequently joined the men in the fields, intending to take over the management of the estate when her father was too old.

Samantha was her only confidant on the subject of marriage. Of the four sisters, Allison had had the fewest prospects.

Rose stood up to pour the tea for her sisters. The most delicate of the sisters, she dreamed away most of her free hours, and longed to travel and see the world. She was an artist, and her hands frequently revealed the leftover stains from her painting. A few years earlier, she'd gone to the coast for formal lessons. Many in Tree Town shook their heads, as higher education for a woman was almost always frowned upon and seemed a great waste if she were to be a wife and keep house. However, the town secretly believed her parents had ulterior motives for sending her away (as any good parent would).

Great was the disappointment of Tree Town when she returned without a proposal.

The next in line was Elizabeth. She was tall, like Allison, but with fair skin and hair. She carried herself with the grace and dignity befitting a queen. Society generally considered her the most beautiful of the sisters.

She was also the most traditional.

While the entire family took a small measure of pride in their willingness to push the boundaries of society, Elizabeth respected those boundaries. If she took pride in anything, it was in her family's achievement of rising above the status of working-class to run in circles of old aristocracy and old money (though she said none of this out loud).

Then there was Victoria (affectionately called Tori by her family). What can be said about Tori? Not very much if you didn't know her, and very few people did. She was shy around strangers, but warm and affectionate with those she was close to.

It may seem that the youngest of five sisters would have a difficult time, yet she was quite content making her own way through life. She held a special place in her father's heart, was petted by her sisters, adored by her few close friends, but altogether went unnoticed by the rest of the world.

They finished tea and would have enjoyed sitting and talking for hours, but Rose had a few items to purchase at the grocers. They waited for Samantha to put on her hat and gloves and walked to the grocers together.

Here I must draw your attention to the simple act of going to the grocers. In a family of wealth and upper class, they would send a servant on such an errand. But the Hartfords had not always been wealthy, and though they now employed household workers, there was no task beneath them. And for this, they often turned heads.

As they were turning heads in that moment, giggling and prancing down the usually quiet Main Street.

Since the wager with Daniel Copeland, Samantha had been attempting to make a list of prospects. Not surprisingly, all the young people in Tree Town had already done their societal duty by securing matches and starting families. Most of the descendants from working class families had long ago settled down—typically at the coast, where there were more jobs available.

William and Daniel were both correct. If they were going to find men, they were going to have to look far and wide.

The sisterly chain stayed linked until it was forced to break at the entrance of the grocers. They made way for the housekeeper of Dr. Vaughn to exit. She was carrying two baskets full of goods, and Allison and Elizabeth quickly helped her load them into her one-horse buggy.

Behind the housekeeper came Mr. Cole, the owner of *Cole & Family Household Goods*. Why it was called *Cole & Family* had always been a mystery since Edward Cole had died young, leaving the business to his wife and only son. The widowed Mrs. Cole was now quite physically impaired. Edward Cole Jr. was the sole owner and manager of the family business, which was never really run by a family at all.

Mr. Cole loaded a large canvas bag of flour into the buggy and bid the housekeeper good day, after good-naturedly receiving all the heaps of compliments and thank-yous she showered upon him.

As she drove away, he turned to the sisters, who were all looking at him with silent laughter dancing on their faces. Flour had escaped from a hole in the bag he had just been carrying, and he was now covered in it. The flour, his prematurely receding hairline, and the way his spectacles perched awkwardly upon his nose made for a comical look. When he gave a small bow and shoved his spectacles further up his nose, the sisters erupted in laughter, which he joined before ushering them inside his store.

"Good day, ladies," Mr. Cole said. "Excuse the appearance. I didn't expect the Hartfords to be coming into town today."

"You should always be prepared," said Allison. "You never know when one of us is going to pop up."

"And one of us lives just a block away, now," said Victoria, looping her arm through Samantha's.

"No longer a Hartford, they tell me," said Mr. Cole, nodding to Samantha. "I apologize I have been unable to call. I congratulate you, and your new husband, and wish you both every happiness."

Samantha thanked him and asked, "How is your mother, Mr. Cole?"

"Don't call me Mr. Cole, anymore, please. Call me Edward. You're a married woman, now."

"May I call you Edward?" asked Victoria.

"Never, Tori. To you, I will always be Mr. Cole." He winked.

"Then you may never call me Tori again." She turned away and pretended to pout.

Elizabeth passed by the counter and said, "Please tell your mother I am looking forward to seeing her on the first of the month."

"She always asks about your pumpkin bread. I've told her repeatedly it is no longer in season," said Mr. Cole.

"I will see if I can find something in our cellar from

last autumn. We may have some cans of pumpkin left."

Mr. Cole assumed his professional stance of grocer and politely asked in what way he could assist the Hartford women in their shopping. Rose went to the counter to show him her list, and he began gathering the wanted items. Samantha looked for a few items for herself.

Allison took up residence near the small collection of books. Victoria idled over to where she was standing near the bookshelf and asked about the open book Allison was holding in her hands. "Is that a romance?"

"I don't read romances," Allison responded. She snapped the book shut and shoved it back onto the shelf.

When the shopping was complete, Victoria and Allison perched themselves on the crate and barrels in the back of the store, though it was highly improper for a young lady to do so in public. Mr. Cole busied himself with dusting some shelves, but kept most of his attention on the five women in his store, intent on serious conversation.

Addressing Allison, he said, "Your father is the most brilliant businessman I know. I think it's wise of him to teach you about it."

"Some people think women can't be business-minded," she said, tossing her head to indicate she thought the notion ridiculous.

"On the contrary. A woman's mind is just as capable as any man's. I would say their emotions, their constitutions, would be more likely to get in the way."

Allison's eyebrows shot up, but she made no reply.

"It's also a little disconcerting," said Elizabeth. "To see a woman ordering men around."

Mr. Cole said, "Just like men with large estates hire other men to carry the burden of overseeing everything, a woman should do the same, if only so the other working men will pay more attention. It's simply common sense."

Victoria cocked her head to the side. Face bunched in confusion, she asked, "If a woman were to hire men to order the men around so she isn't doing it herself, then who would order *those* men around?"

During the conversation, Samantha remained quiet and observant. Mr. Cole was a bachelor. He'd always been a bachelor. He was quite the elder brother to the Hartford sisters, and he'd always seemed—well—brotherly.

However, if she were going to win this wager, she needed to ensure she didn't overlook any possibility. So she paired each of the sisters with him in her mind.

Rose was delicate and full of dreams. Samantha couldn't see her happy being tied down to the grocers.

Allison—no—Allison would not do. Far too headstrong for Mr. Cole. Besides, she'd once declared herself a spinster for life so she might be free to manage their father's estate (an obstacle Samantha knew would be overcome once Allison fell deeply in love).

Elizabeth was too fashionable, and they'd always imagined her marrying some aristocrat or prince or heir to a fortune.

Victoria—Victoria seemed much too young for Mr. Cole.

Samantha sighed. Once her sisters were all engaged, she'd have to turn her thoughts to finding a wife for Mr. Cole.

The bell attached to the storefront door rang to announce a customer. Allison and Victoria hopped off the barrels, and Mr. Cole immediately assumed his business demeanor and went to the counter to see to Mrs. Evans's needs. She was looking for a certain type of rare nut that Mr. Cole informed her he did not carry in the store. In fact, he had never heard of the nut. She then began a long dissertation informing him of how the nut was discovered by Christopher Columbus and was widely used in dishes around Europe.

The sisters, knowing the conversation with Mr. Cole was over, exited the store while waving apologetically to Mr. Cole.

The walk towards Samantha's home was slower than the walk to the store. The setting sun signaled the day's end, and the sisters determined to hold on to every last bit of light before they parted ways.

"Did I tell you we will be having a visitor?" asked Samantha (though she was quite aware she had yet to mention anything about it).

"Who is coming?" asked Elizabeth.

"His name is Reuben Dudley. He's a school friend of William's. We invited him to visit us for a short holiday before he begins work with the shipping yard."

"Are you going to bring him to call on us?" asked Rose.

"Of course," said Samantha. "I thought you all could help me entertain him. I think he'll enjoy your company."

"How old is he?" asked Rose.

"I believe he's William's age. Twenty-six," Samantha answered.

"Is he handsome?" asked Elizabeth.

"I've never met him," said Samantha (though William had already informed her Reuben was notably handsome).

"I suppose that is one pity about not having a large wedding," remarked Elizabeth. "You didn't get to meet any of William's friends."

"I suppose that's one reason William suggested Reuben come to stay with us." Samantha was determined not to give anything away.

At the door of Samantha's home, she gave each of her sisters a kiss and stood on the doorstep, waving goodbye until they were out of sight. She smiled to herself as she passed into the foyer, thinking how enjoyable the next few weeks were sure to be.

3

He Will Probably Be Ugly

The Hartford sisters were trying to suppress their excitement as they helped their mother and the cook prepare for their evening meal with Samantha, William, and the mysterious Reuben Dudley. The house—usually lively in all respects—was unusually frenzied as the girls shot up and down the stairs, changing outfits, redoing hair, and exclaiming, "Is that the time already?"

The Hartfords had evening supper guests and afternoon tea guests and Sunday morning breakfast guests frequently enough, so why was this visit causing such a flurry of anticipation?

If your sister and her husband were bringing to supper a young, unattached man of good employment, you might find yourself a little anxious as well. While the sisters were used to encountering society at the coast, it was rare for society to come to Tree Town. (Though one man could hardly be called "society.")

Reuben Dudley was also causing a flurry of excitement throughout Tree Town. Upon his arrival, Samantha immediately cursed herself for not having the forethought of putting Reuben up at her family's home. It was much larger, it would have given Reuben more time with her sisters, and it was far away from the prying eyes of the town.

Prying eyes who couldn't resist dropping by every hour to inquire after Samantha's health.

It was with great difficulty that Samantha and William were able to extricate themselves from their home in time for supper at the Hartfords. They opted to take a carriage, though walking was their usual means of transportation, if only so they would less likely be detained by a curious person seeking to know who was the handsome man—with dark hair and features and a broad jaw—accompanying the Temples.

On their way, they passed Daniel Copeland idling down Main Street. He glanced up, took in the stranger in the carriage, and saluted Samantha with a tip of his hat.

Samantha flushed, then acknowledged him with a demure nod, reminding herself he was bound to secrecy (a rule of the wager) regarding the real reason for Reuben's visit. She smiled to herself as they neared the Hartford estate. Reuben was the strong, silent, handsome sort, and she felt sure at least one of her sisters would fall in love with him.

Mrs. Hartford was a practical woman. It was credit to her that her daughters rarely let their heads run away with thoughts of young men or suitors or the general frivolity often found in society. She wanted her daughters equipped with every advantage, knowing full well the world was a harsh place for unmarried women.

Because she was a practical woman, she also paid special attention to the meal preparations, more so than if William and Samantha had been the only supper guests.

With only the finishing touches remaining, Mrs. Hartford ushered her daughters into the parlor to rest before the guests arrived. The sisters sank into separate chairs and quietly composed themselves.

Then Rose spoke. "He will probably be ugly," she said, as though it didn't matter at all.

"Yes, just our luck," said Elizabeth. (It did matter to her.)

"Why does it matter?" asked Victoria.

The other sisters looked at her. She shrugged innocently. "I was just asking," she said.

Elizabeth went to the piano and began to play. The piece she chose was entitled *Reverie.* It was slow and melodramatic, telling a tale of tragic love of which only memories remained. Victoria yawned. Rose got out her needlepoint and began to stitch frantically. Allison rescued them by saying, "Why don't you play something else? Do you want us to be unconscious when the guest arrives?"

Elizabeth opened her mouth to protest, but a knock on the front door and a creak of the hinges announced Samantha and William had arrived.

"Halloo family!" called Samantha. In they came. First Samantha, then William, followed by the mystery man.

He was tall, dark, and to everyone's delight, very handsome.

The sisters stood and were introduced to Mr. Dudley. One by one, he greeted them. Just when he'd finished saying, "How do you do?" to Victoria, Mrs. Hartford entered. She gave Samantha and William each a kiss, greeted the guest, and announced supper. As she turned toward the door to lead the way to the dining room, she glanced over her shoulder and raised her eyebrows at her daughters, who stood neatly in a row.

This brought forth a giggle from Victoria, a smile from Elizabeth, a roll of the eyes from Allison, and a good-humored shake of her head from Rose.

Samantha saw the whole thing and beamed all the way to supper. She thought this might not be so difficult after all.

The evening came.

The evening went.

Rose and Allison will tell you their opinions.

Allison went to Rose's room as she was preparing to sleep. Rose sat at the vanity and Allison sat on the edge of the bed. In the candlelight, they began to discuss their new acquaintance.

"He was very serious," said Rose.

"But very handsome," said Allison. "His beauty almost made up for his lack of conversation." After staring at the coverlet for a few seconds she said,

"He'd be perfect for Elizabeth."

"He hardly said a word to any of us." Rose finished putting her hair in curlers and crawled onto the bed next to Allison. "He only spoke with Mother and Father and William. He said a little to Samantha, I guess."

"Perhaps women make him shy," Allison suggested.

"We are quite a lot to handle. But tonight, you could hear every clink of china. I quite forgot how to speak. But it wasn't so very awkward, was it?"

Allison pinched her lips. "I think it was every bit of awkward. I just wonder if Mr. Dudley noticed. He doesn't know us, after all."

Rose yawned and stretched. "Poor Samantha. I hope he's more engaging when he's with her and William. He'll be here for two whole weeks. What a bore that will be."

"She asked us to help entertain him. Perhaps we should draw straws?"

"Don't be mean."

"You're the one who said he was boring."

"I said he was serious." Rose clasped her hands over her knees. "And we should certainly take turns so as to not overwhelm him."

Allison stood to leave. "Yes, yes. Heaven help the poor bloke who comes in contact with the devastating torrent of Hartford sisters."

Rose sniggered into her hand, then she sat up straight. "Do you think Samantha and William brought him here on purpose? To—make a match?"

Allison laughed. "All the wedding and marriage business with our older sister has gone to your head. I suppose it could have gone to Samantha's as well.

But I can't imagine her doing such a thing without telling us."

Rose shrugged and lay back on her pillow.

Allison raised her candle in salute as she departed, and they said no more on the subject for the duration of Reuben Dudley's stay in Tree Town.

Every occasion that Reuben Dudley spent any time with the Hartfords, it was always the same. He conversed easily with Mr. Hartford and Mrs. Hartford, but when it came to the unmarried Hartford women, he barely said a word. Eventually, Allison became indignant. Elizabeth and Rose were confused and a little disappointed. Victoria simply enjoyed having Samantha and William around more often. William never ignored Samantha's sisters and always appeared to enjoy their company. You might have believed he'd always been a part of the family.

Unfortunately for any future suitors who might pursue another sister, William had raised the standard quite high.

Mr. Dudley came.

Mr. Dudley went.

He left with cordial goodbyes and well-wishes to the family, but it was no surprise at the end of his two-week stay in Tree Town that there was no tearful, heart-breaking goodbye on the side of any Hartford sisters. Their lives returned to normal without any suspicion regarding how disappointed the whole affair had left William and Samantha.

The day that Mr. Dudley left was not yet over when Daniel Copeland visited Samantha, prancing proudly and practically crowing. But, he was cautious in the way he began his gloating (he was not a complete scoundrel). He tested out Samantha's countenance first.

Once seated in the Temple's tiny parlor, with a teacup cradled in his palm, he said, "I hear you had a visitor these past few weeks." He watched Samantha's face closely.

"Yes, I think most everyone in town had a chance to meet Mr. Dudley," Samantha replied, with no sign of vexation.

"It's a pity I didn't have the opportunity," Daniel said, staring at the ceiling above Samantha's head.

Samantha wanted to say, "You had plenty of opportunity but conveniently managed to avoid us," but she didn't.

Daniel could resist no longer. "Well? Do I hear wedding bells? Or was your first attempt to find a match a failure?" he asked.

Samantha quelled her frustration before she replied evenly, "It was not a complete failure, but there are no wedding bells."

Daniel smiled triumphantly and nearly jostled the tea out of his cup. He placed it carefully on the table tray and said, "I knew you were up to something when I saw that man going about with you. It didn't take your family long to run him off, did it?"

Suddenly, Samantha was fighting to suppress her laughter. "We didn't run him off, Daniel. He left of his own accord. There were no sparks between him or any of my sisters. But this does not entirely indicate that there will be none in the future."

"It only indicates that there will be none in the *near* future, hence your first attempt was a failure."

Samantha sighed. "It's true no attachment was formed, but I learned a great deal and will be better prepared next time."

Daniel smirked. "Pray tell me what you learned. Or is it against the rules of warfare to share your tactics with the enemy?"

"You are not my enemy, and I *will* tell you what I learned. I learned not to have expectations. One cannot control a heart, merely guide the circumstances. Next time, I'll do what I can and wait patiently for results, knowing all the while things may not turn out the way I hope they will."

Daniel raised his eyebrows and was silent for a moment. Samantha thought she might have reached a more thoughtful, conscientious part of him, as he appeared to mull over her words.

However, no profound thought produced itself when next he spoke. "All I will say is, I believe I am right and will triumph in the end. This episode has only heightened my confidence. When I saw your Mr. Dudley, I thought perhaps I should take a stand on the offense. After this, I think your battle was lost before it began."

Samantha resisted the urge to retort, saying calmly, "You may be right, but all will be well in the end no matter what the outcome."

Daniel gave a nod, said goodbye, and left quickly.

That night, Samantha prayed very hard for a miracle.

4

Perfectly Dull, But Not Pointless

The Temple's disappointment that no attachment had been formed between Mr. Dudley and one of the sisters lasted for several days. Compounding this disappointment was the reality Samantha and William were momentarily stumped for more prospects.

William thought seriously about demanding Reuben marry a sister as terms of his new position as bookkeeper. But alas, time enough remained for more suitors. The trouble was finding them. Who would they bring to Tree Town next?

It might satisfy you to hear, an answer to Samantha's desperate prayer following Daniel Copeland's gloating visit was already on its way. The man in question was a long forgotten old friend who arrived in Tree Town just as the disappointed hopes of the sad couple were subsiding.

Upon a lazy Sunday afternoon, Samantha was in the parlor, reading a book entitled *Anthology of Anthropological Findings from the Eighteenth*

Century. William, having just returned from a business visit to the coast, relaxed near her as he read a book entitled *Nautical Terms.* There was a rap on the door and Samantha, believing it to be one of her sisters, quickly rose to attend to it.

She found the figure of a strange man, standing on the front step and facing the street, taking in the view of Tree Town. When he turned around, smiled and said, "I heard my favorite sister had gotten married," she was struck with recollection and broke into a gleeful grin as she embraced the no longer strange visitor.

"Ethan!" she gasped. "You are finally home. It has been so long!" She pulled him through the doorway with exclamations at how much he had changed and how happy she was to see him.

He laughed with her. "I was surprised when my aunt wrote and said you were married—happy surprise, of course—I said the first thing I would do when I reached Tree Town, would be find Samantha and meet her lucky man." Ethan grinned widely as he was half pulled, half pushed, into the parlor.

When they entered, William was on his feet, prepared to meet the person who was causing such a ruckus. He held out his hand as Samantha made the introductions.

"Dear, this is Ethan Clay," said Samantha. She moved to her husband's side and wrapped her arm around his middle.

Both men said, "How do you do?" and appraised each other pleasantly.

"Ethan is an old friend," said Samantha. "He was

practically family once. He worked for my father and was as much a brother to us Hartford sisters as anyone could have been." She focused on Ethan. "Now Ethan, I hope my husband will meet with your approval. You are one of few people whose opinion I value."

"I've already formed my opinion," said Ethan, as they took their seats. "I decided if he met with your approval, then I am determined to like him." Then he said, as he directed his eyes to William, "And I know I shall."

William, in turn, gave Ethan a nod of approval. He had been suffering under Tree Town scrutiny, and it was a fresh breeze to acquaint someone who did not require proof of sanity or have a preconceived judgment.

During this exchange, Samantha absorbed the change that had occurred in Ethan. He had grown only a little taller (he had been quite tall when she'd last seen him). His dark hair was longer (it suited him). His chin was covered in stubble, making him look very grown up. He'd filled out quite nicely, every shred of boyish features gone, except for his eyes, which still danced with the mischief of concocting schemes and getting into trouble.

"Ethan, tell us of your adventures—I cannot believe it has been five years." Samantha leaned forward eagerly.

"Nothing but books, books, books, and more books. Perfectly dull, but not pointless. I learned a great deal." Ethan was still grinning at the evidence of happiness sitting before him.

"Did you do any traveling abroad?" asked William.

"Only once. I went to Rome for a summer."

"How did you find it?"

"Big. Too big for my taste, but I enjoyed the catacombs. I visited them seven times. Have you ever been?"

"Yes," said William.

"He's been several times," said Samantha. "Every time before we were married. He's promised to take me there one day. I cannot wait to see it."

"You will love it," said Ethan. "You should take Rose with you. I could see her fitting in there."

When he said this, a little voice inside of Samantha whispered, *How would you know what Rose would like? You haven't been around for five years.* But she silenced it and spoke animatedly when Ethan turned the conversation away from himself by inquiring into the events leading up to Samantha and William's marriage. They told him the story they had told so many times, but with added details they felt only a close friend would appreciate.

"My aunt's telling was not quite so amusing," Ethan said. "I'm glad to have the account straight from the source."

"Who is your aunt?" asked William.

"I apologize, love, I forgot to tell you," said Samantha. "Ethan is the nephew of Loretta Humphrey. The one we call Aunt Letty."

"She's a dear old soul," said Ethan. "She raised me since I was five, when my parents died of influenza. But not without the help of the very generous and loving Hartford family. We would never have lasted without their aid." Ethan's eyes twinkled with the rekindling of fond memories.

"Have you seen Aunt Letty yet?" asked Samantha.

"Yes, she met me at the station. She knew I wanted to see you so she promised to have supper waiting and we will eat our meal together just as we always did."

"Then you haven't seen my family yet?"

Ethan shook his head.

"Do they know you are home?" Samantha inquired.

"I assume my aunt has told them." Ethan's grin had subsided to a quiet smile.

"Well, I suppose someone will pose the question eventually, but why in the world did we not hear from you? Nor did you come to visit, the entire time you were away?" Samantha playfully reprimanded him in the older-sister tone she was skilled at adopting when the need arose.

Ethan hesitated. "I imagined Aunt Letty passed on all the news."

"She did, from time to time," said Samantha.

"Did she tell you I will be working for your father again?" asked Ethan.

Samantha sat forward in surprise. "You mean, doing what you did before you left?"

"That is correct."

"But why? You have your education, your experience, you could do whatever you wanted."

"Ah, but you forget—no name, no connections, and no money. Those are important assets in this world."

"I'm sure you could find some other employment you enjoy."

"That's exactly it. I always enjoyed working on the estate. If it hadn't been for your father's encouragement in the first place, I would never have gone to school. Now I will be back doing what I had always wanted to do, but with more experience, more knowledge, and more assurance it's what I really want."

Samantha smiled. "I am proud of you, Ethan. You have grown up nicely. I know my entire family will be overjoyed to have you in their lives once more."

Ethan remarked it was getting late, and Aunt Letty would be waiting for him. He said goodbye with a firm handshake for William and a kiss for Samantha and sauntered confidently off in search of his childhood home.

After he was gone, Samantha erupted in excitement. She hugged William, exclaiming that all hope was not lost. "It has been so long that I had forgotten all about him!"

"Yes, tell me why he never married one of your sisters."

"I believe there was some leaning in that direction," said Samantha. "But something happened before he left. We still aren't sure what. It's quite a mystery. One day, he disappeared. Father said he had gone to school and would likely not be returning.

"We were all devastated, of course. I told you how much he meant to us. It wasn't until a few weeks after his departure that I began to understand part of the reason for his leaving."

"What happened?" asked William.

"Well, he was especially fond of Allison. There were

times we suspected a bit of an attachment. When Ethan left, Allison was quite downcast. We all noticed a change in her. Eventually she revealed the whole story to me, but she made me promise not to tell anyone."

William sighed, disappointed, but willing to respect the confidence maintained between sisters.

Samantha, however, did not consider her husband "anyone."

"Allow me to make a pot of tea," said Samantha. "Then I will tell you a sad tale that may yet have a happy ending."

5

Why Don't You Knit More Often?

We have already heard from Ethan that he was an orphan. Considering his aunt resided near the Hartfords, and Mr. and Mrs. Hartford took seriously the Christian mandate to visit widows and orphans, and that the financial situation of Aunt Letty and her newly acquired ward was less than substantial, it is not strange that Ethan would have spent a great deal of his boyhood working and playing beside the five Hartford sisters.

Aside from the usual skirmishes between children, Ethan was altogether adored by his adopted sisters. He, in turn, adored them, but one sister was his particularly close friend.

Allison was free in the outdoors. She enjoyed climbing trees, swimming, and long hours spent working in the fields. In those days, her conduct was less than acceptable in the eyes of the world. Her adventures were uncommon and looked down upon for a young lady. It was improper for her to have her skirts hiked up to her waist as she plowed a low field or to be seen too much out of doors at all.

Young girls were expected to be calm, quiet, and dignified. They learned to needlepoint, to sing and dance, and to be proper and mild-mannered. It was one thing for Allison to defy these female accomplishments. It was quite another for her parents to do nothing to curtail her.

Mr. Hartford believed labor of the hands was good employment for boys and girls alike. All the daughters were involved in the management and daily workings of the estate, but Allison took to the task more readily than the others. Her health and happiness extinguished any doubt the Hartford parents may have had about allowing her to roam so freely.

Her disposition was such that she did not mind when she was often excluded from female society anywhere she went. While Samantha and Rose were invited to parties and to have tea—the invitations nearly always left off Allison's name.

These realities meant Ethan and Allison were frequently in each other's company. Allison enjoyed teasing and tormenting Ethan. Ethan always considered it his duty to accept with patience the torment she inflicted upon him, though inwardly he enjoyed her teasing and was lonely when her household duties kept her from the fields. (But he would never own it.) He would goad her to stay longer by saying things such as, "Why don't you knit more often? It might improve you. Besides, don't you find this work too difficult?"

She would retort, "Why don't you try knitting? You

will find that it isn't very easy. Anyone can use a spade. It takes skill to wield a needle."

Ethan would ask, "If you are so intelligent and skilled, why do you insist on spending so much time in the fields?"

On the banter would go until they were laughing at some new distraction, and the days would pass quickly.

Ethan and Allison had a happy, carefree childhood before the fateful summer when something changed between them. Neither knew exactly what happened, they only knew when it happened.

It was the evening of Allison's seventeenth birthday. Ethan told her he had a surprise for her, but he would only give it to her if she met him by the brook, near a certain spot, around midnight.

Whether Ethan really had a surprise or not made no difference to Allison. He understood her tendency for mischief better than anyone. The thrill of escaping from the house unnoticed would alone make the scheme worth doing.

The first time a person attempts to make an escape from their own bedroom window is always a bit frightening. As Allison sat dangling her feet over the edge of the roof, staring into darkness, she almost returned to the comfort of her bed. However, the thought of Ethan waiting by the brook, wondering if she truly had the courage to attempt it, gave her new strength. She propelled herself forth and landed in a heap on the lawn.

When Allison pulled herself to standing, she was startled by a shuffling of feet and garbled laughter.

She whirled toward it. From behind the dogwood in the back of the house, Ethan appeared. He was grinning from ear to ear. He put a finger to his lips to silence any exclamation from her, and they both hurried away into the night.

The moon lit their way down the lane toward the brook. Ethan led her purposefully toward a grove of trees. When they reached it, they sank, breathless, onto the mossy bank.

The trees blocked most of the moonlight, but just enough pushed its way through to form a reflection on the water, giving sufficient light.

"I didn't think you'd do it," Ethan said.

She said, "Well, you were wrong."

"Yes, I suppose I was. Did I scare you?"

"No."

"Yes I did. I saw you jump."

"You startled me. I didn't expect you to be waiting."

"I would never miss a show like that. And you have to admit, it was fun."

"It was fun, but don't act like it was all your idea."

"It *was* my idea."

"But I *did* it. You just watched."

"All right. But do you want to know what your surprise is? You deserve it after a stunt like that." Ethan stood and withdrew an object from behind a tree.

He brought the lump to her and sank to his knees at her side. It was wrapped in a blanket, and as he placed it in her lap he said, somewhat shyly, "I hope you like it."

Allison unfolded the blanket to find a wooden box.

She could smell cedar. As she swept her hands over the smoothly carved wood, she asked, "What is it?"

"A box," said Ethan.

"Yes, what is it for?"

"To keep treasures in."

"What sort of treasures?"

"Anything you want."

Allison opened it and felt the smooth, flawless wood on the inside. "You made this?" she asked.

"Yes. You can't see it very well, but your name is carved into the top. Just in case someone tries to take it from you."

Suddenly, all the brash insults that accompanied any conversation between herself and Ethan disappeared. She was speechless.

"Do you like it?" Ethan's voice was tense with anticipation.

"I love it," Allison managed to whisper. "This—this wasn't at all what I was expecting."

"What were you expecting?"

"I don't know. Maybe that you would get me out here and laugh at all the trouble I went through."

"I would never do that to you."

The seriousness of his tone caused Allison to look up. She held his gaze and marveled at how much time he must have put into making the box.

Ethan shook his head to clear it. "Just don't show it to anyone," he said. "I don't want your sisters to get jealous."

Allison closed the lid of the box, and set it to the side. "I do believe you have made this my favorite birthday ever." Slowly, she scooted toward him and gave him a kiss on the cheek.

Ethan started, and sat back on the moss. Then he broke into a wide smile. He stood and pulled her to her feet. "I'll make you a hundred boxes if that's the reaction I get." Then he turned away and walked quickly out of the woods and toward the footbridge that crossed the stream.

When he reached the bridge, Allison called to him, "Wait, aren't you going to walk me home?"

"You know the way. Don't get too scared." He grinned at her, and then ran into the darkness.

Allison only smiled and began to make her way back home. As she neared the house, her thoughts changed from the evening's events to one thing that she had forgotten: how in the world was she to get back inside?

Although Ethan told Allison to show the box to no one, she couldn't resist letting Samantha in on the secret. Samantha was as amazed as Allison at the skill that went into its making. If either girl had an inclination the box suggested warm feelings from the giver, they did not discuss it then.

The summer continued as every summer before it had. Ethan and Allison worked hard together in the cool of the morning and in the evenings. In the afternoons, when the heat and humidity became oppressive, they would relax by the brook, in the same place where Ethan gave the gift to Allison.

They were not always alone. The other sisters

worked consistently, but no one would deny Ethan and Allison, together, had a gift for running the estate.

Sunday was a day of leisure. Hence it was a Saturday night tradition for the Hartford girls to spend the evenings reading on the veranda. As the sun would sink, they would gather up a few old quilts from the house and walk to a grassy, unplowed field. The field was the only untouched portion of land on the estate, as it was the only hill in that whole part of the county. At the peak of the hill, one could look down upon the Hartford home, with a backdrop of the countryside stretching for miles.

Ethan would nearly always join the girls and all six of them would lie on their quilts, talking, laughing, and telling stories late into the evening.

On one of these Saturdays, when they were all walking home, Ethan and Allison hung back from the rest of the group. Ethan whispered to Allison, "Did you enjoy sneaking out on your birthday?"

Allison grinned. "Yes, I did."

"Do you want to do it again tonight?"

Allison nodded. "Meet you there?"

"As soon as you can. I'll be waiting." Ethan called "goodnight!" to the other girls and ran toward the small cottage where he lived with Aunt Letty.

Allison was anxious as she lay, fully clothed, in her bed, waiting for the house to quiet down and then allowing sufficient time for everyone to fall asleep. Once she was sure all was safe, she opened her window, tossing a rope she'd prepared to make her return easier (she'd nearly woken the whole house on that first night when she'd had to sneak in through the kitchens).

The night was brighter than it had been on the evening of her birthday. A figure again appeared from behind the dogwood. She was pleased Ethan was not so immature as to try and scare her once again.

Her landing was as muddled as the first one had been. Ethan was at her side the instant she hit the ground. He grinned broadly as he extended his hand to help her up, and they both started off for the place by the brook that had become their spot.

For the rest of the summer, sneaking out of bedroom windows and enjoying talks by the brook also became a Saturday night ritual.

When first these excursions began, Allison thought little of the impropriety of it all. However, she experienced one pang of guilt that she could not leave unheeded for long.

Samantha had always been her confidant. Allison felt in some small way that she was betraying Samantha by having secret meetings with Ethan without telling her. After a few weeks of consternation—she did not know how Samantha would react when she found out—Allison told her older sister about every rendezvous with Ethan.

Samantha didn't quite know what to think of it. She was afraid Allison and Ethan were growing too close. Where would their friendship lead? How long would they continue in this way? She posed her concern to her sister and left the result up to Allison, ending with the question of whether or not their parents would approve of nighttime meetings with a young man unchaperoned.

Allison protested that Ethan was only a brother.

Both young ladies were quite aware this was no longer true (though neither of them voiced this at the time).

Allison had no time to analyze her actions and involvement with Ethan. One day, he did not come to work. She assumed he was sick, though she was surprised no one had sent word or informed her of the reason for his absence.

That evening, Mr. Hartford called the family together. He informed them solemnly that Ethan had received—from an anonymous benefactor—the means to attend university. He was gone, and would not be returning.

The suddenness of his departure struck deeply, but it affected Allison the most. She fled the house, escaping into the woods until night had fallen. Later, Samantha found her in her room, sobbing.

"He didn't say goodbye," Allison blurted out.

Samantha could only hug her. They were all sad to lose him so quickly, but Samantha was also a little angry, feeling it very rude of him to disappear without saying a word.

Several weeks passed. Life trickled back to normal. Only Ethan was missing. Everyone did their best to adjust, yet Allison seemed permanently altered— quieter, and much less jovial.

On a Saturday evening, when a little violet and orange sunlight hung in the sky, Allison wandered away from the house. Samantha, on impulse, followed after her. She found Allison sitting by the brook, on a mossy spot beneath the trees at the beginning of the wood. Samantha sat beside her and asked what was troubling her.

Allison exhaled. Her voice quivered when she spoke. "I think you were right," she said. Her face was pale and drawn. "I think you were right when you said Ethan and I were growing close. I knew we were. The two of us—we weren't like the rest of you." A tear rolled down her cheek, but she didn't bother to brush it away. She sat in silence and swallowed a few deep sobs.

Samantha braced herself for the confession she knew was coming. She could only ache for her sister as she wrapped an arm around her shoulders and hugged her close.

"I think," said Allison. She hesitated just a moment longer. "I think that I loved him."

6

I'm Sure There's An Explanation

Back in the parlor of Samantha and William's home, William sighed deeply when Samantha had completed her tale. He shook his head slowly and stared straight ahead, half dazed. "I find it nearly unbelievable," he said.

"Yes, I know," said Samantha. "It's a bit scandalous even for our family."

"No, I find it nearly unbelievable that you were so kind to him. What a dolt—for leaving like that and not saying a word. I cannot believe your father is now offering him a position on the estate, after he treated your family so."

Samantha refilled her cup of tea. "It makes me think there is more to the story."

"Did you ever ask your father about it?"

"Honestly, it never occurred to me. He was deeply saddened—almost as much as we all were. I suppose I assumed Ethan had abandoned him as well. But— yes, there must be more to the story. Did you hear

Ethan say my father encouraged him to go to school?"

William crossed his arms and propped one foot on the tea table. "You think he knew about Allison's—affection?"

Samantha tapped her finger on her cup. "I wonder..."

"Well, if I know Allison at all, I'll be surprised if she is as forbearing as you, dear."

"She can be rather hot-headed. But if there is still anything between them, I'm sure she will forgive him."

"Challenge or no challenge, I hope she doesn't forgive him too quickly."

"He certainly has a lot of explaining to do."

"Pity. I really liked the bloke."

Samantha laughed. "He's still the same person. Come to think of it, if he'd felt guilty for his disappearance, I doubt he'd have been quite so eager to come see us."

William tapped his chin with a finger. "Curious. I wish you'd drilled him with more questions."

Samantha placed her teacup on the table. "We can be sure my family has that part well in hand."

At the Hartford estate, Allison was in her father's study, going over the ledgers from the quarter. An item had appeared in the box titled "wages." Knowing her father must have placed it there, she carried the ledger out into the hallway. "Father," she called. No response came, so she called again.

That's when she heard the laughter of two men

coming from the parlor. Who could be visiting at this time of night?

Allison strode toward the voices. When she entered the front room, she was struck dumb immediately.

Ethan Clay stood up the moment he saw her. Though his appearance had altered considerably in five years, he was very much the boy she'd known from her childhood—with the same devilishly handsome grin that suggested all sorts of mischief. He held his hat in his hands and began twisting it about. "Allison," he said after a short while.

Allison stammered, but no intelligible words came forth.

"Darling," Mr. Hartford interjected. He rose from his seat also.

Allison shifted her gaze to him and slowly she began to realize the reason for the added box beneath "wages" on the ledger.

This realization caused a surge of hot anger, as her father had apparently forgotten to inform her they would be taking on a new man (never mind they'd discussed, on a dozen occasions, the hiring of several employees for the coming quarter).

Not only had he neglected to inform her, he'd conveniently left out the part about Ethan coming home.

Seeing the signs of a storm brewing, Mr. Hartford held out a hand to Ethan. "Shall I see you in the morning, then?"

Ethan shook the offered hand, but did not remove his eyes from Allison.

Allison snapped the ledger shut. As a thousand

thoughts raced through her mind, she couldn't formulate any of them into something remotely dignified. She would rather die than lose her temper in front of Ethan Samuel Clay. She'd have a conversation with her father later.

With that, she pivoted on her heels and went directly out the front door.

Allison plowed down the country road leading to town. It was late, but she was sure Samantha and William would not have retired yet. She had to speak to someone, and she couldn't remain in the house.

Her arms swung at her sides as she marched down Main Street. The streets were empty, and lights flickered in the windows as Tree Town prepared to sleep, little suspecting a ferocious tiger prowled outside.

Allison rapped on the door of Samantha's home. The minute she'd completed the act, she nearly turned and ran. What was she doing? Calling at such an hour—and over such a silly thing?

Her self-consciousness abated when William opened the door. "Allison?" his face registered concern.

"I must speak with my sister." Allison pushed passed him, down the hall, and into the parlor where Samantha was cleaning up the tea tray. Briefly, Allison wondered why they were having tea at that time of night. She took a gulp of air as Samantha asked, "Allison, what is the matter?"

William passed by the door to the parlor and silently motioned to Samantha that he would be in the next room.

"He's back," Allison said. "Ethan Clay is back. And he didn't say a word to me. And Father has hired him. And Father didn't tell me." Allison started to sit in one of the armchairs but flew up the moment her rump hit the cushion. "What is he thinking, just waltzing back here without so much as one word for five years? And Father, what is he thinking, making a hire without speaking to me first?"

From her perch on the sofa, Samantha watched Allison pace back and forth. Once the torrent had passed, Samantha said, "Darling, why on earth is that such a bad thing? You and Ethan were always good friends."

Allison rounded on her. "We were! Which is why this is all so ridiculous."

Samantha reached for the teapot to pour herself another cup, then shook it when she realized it was empty (she and William having polished off the contents just before Allison arrived). She placed the pot down again and said, "I'm sure there is a very good reason for all of this. Though I'm surprised Father didn't inform you of Ethan's return. Does he always consult you before making new hires?"

Allison simmered slightly, but continued to pace. "No, not always. We discuss the need and the funds—which we did this quarter—but that is entirely beside the point. He should have definitely told me if he were planning to hire Ethan Clay."

"I agree. But perhaps he planned to tell you?"

"Planning and doing are completely different things. And Ethan...what is he thinking, just showing up after five years?"

"I'm sure there's an explanation."

"Well, he's going to have to come to me. I'll not go to him. If he's going to be a stranger for so long, then I intend to treat him like one."

At such a moment, William re-entered the parlor. "I forgot my—" He pointed at the table where his bills and letters lay abandoned. He saw Allison's face and queried, "Everything all right?"

As if every man in the world were to blame, Allison glared at William. Her fists were bunched so tight at her side, it seemed she might explode. Instead, she threw her hands into the air, declared "Gah" (much meaning was contained in that word), and marched straight out of the house.

Samantha stood to watch her go.

Eyes wide, William said, "I take it things aren't going so well."

But Samantha clapped her hands. "Things are going splendidly. You were right though, I don't think Allison will forgive him easily." She sank back onto the sofa.

"Are you—going to intervene? Try and smooth things over?" William asked.

"Oh not for the world!" Samantha laughed. "I will simply put up my feet and watch what happens."

"She can't possibly still love him, then?"

Samantha chuckled. "Oh, I believe she's very in love with him. She wouldn't be half so angry if she weren't!"

William shook his head, bewildered. But seeing as the storm had passed and it was safe to be in his own parlor, he returned to it gingerly. As he took up his papers, he thought there wasn't a man he pitied more than Ethan Clay.

God help any person who fell into the path of Allison's fury.

7

Nothing But Silence For Five Whole Years

Mr. Hartford had every reason to believe Allison would be offended at having not been consulted about Ethan's hire.

Why then did he proceed with such a plan?

He had never claimed to be a very wise man. Only a little wise. But somewhere deep in his gut, he knew Ethan was the right choice.

However, he began to doubt his instincts when, first thing in the morning, Allison plowed into his study, eyes blazing.

It had been a very long time since he'd seen her quite so angry.

It was an ambush. "Father, did you hire Ethan Clay without speaking with me?" She propped her knuckles on his desk as she glared down at him.

Mr. Hartford proceeded carefully. "Why, I suppose I invited him home without speaking with you. But the formal hire has not been made. He comes this morning, and I thought we'd all sit down and talk it over."

Allison stood and crossed her arms. "Did you think perhaps I might like a say in this? *Without* him sitting in the same room?"

Mr. Hartford had a sensation similar to the one from his school days, when he'd been caught in a trespass. He swallowed. "Do you not wish to hire him?"

"It's too late, you've already invited him."

"Yes, but if you do not wish to hire him—it would cause a great disappointment to be sure—but, might I know the reason? You were always good friends, and he was always a hard worker. I didn't think you'd disapprove. Did I misjudge the situation?"

She dropped her arms, exasperated. "*Why* did you not ask me?"

Mr. Hartford sat forward, resting his elbows on his desk. "My daughter, the decision is yours. If you wish for me to withdraw the offer, I will do so at once."

Slightly subdued, Allison squared her shoulders. "Hartfords do not break promises. I'm merely disappointed I was not consulted."

"Then I apologize and it will never happen again."

Allison nodded absently, and turned to leave.

When she reached the door, Mr. Hartford inquired. "Allison, if I had consulted you before making the offer, what would you have said?"

Allison gave a noncommittal "Hmm" sound as she stared at the ceiling. Then she departed without an answer.

Mr. Hartford leaned back and picked up The Post, but his vision blurred as he stared at the headline. He'd offered Ethan temporary employment, though he fully intended to extend that offer if Ethan still found the work suited him.

As it were, his instincts also told him Allison's displeasure was warranted, but not because she had not been consulted about Ethan's hire.

He smiled and opened The Post, propping his feet up on the desk.

His instincts told him hiring Ethan was a very good decision.

Ethan had imagined what it would be like to see Allison again. He'd imagined it so many times, leading up to his return to Tree Town. He'd met her in his mind a hundred ways—in the fields, in her family's home, at their spot by the brook. For five years, he dreaded the day Aunt Letty would write to him, informing him Allison had married. He dreaded it so much, his hands shook each time he opened a letter.

But by and by, no word of an attachment ever reached him. Once he'd accepted Mr. Hartford's offer to return for a temporary duration to the Hartford estate, he couldn't stop dreaming about the opportunity for a second chance.

In all of his imaginings, never once did he imagine how it really happened.

First, seeing Allison in her father's home nearly took his breath away. Though it wasn't polished or perfect, it confirmed his feelings had not abated. If anything, they returned in such a rush of ardor he'd barely slept that night. He'd always thought her pretty (though most people did not consider Allison as attractive as her sisters). But the moment he saw her in the parlor, she immediately moved from pretty to so handsome he lost all capacity to think or speak.

He was so enraptured, he whistled to himself the following morning when he returned to the grounds for his formal induction as employee.

The first Hartford he encountered that morning was Mrs. Hartford, who shed all propriety and ran outdoors when she spotted him approaching. She hugged him like he was her own son. Her eyes were misty when she released him, and he felt a warm globe—like sunlight—in the pit of his stomach when he realized he hadn't been alone in missing the Hartfords. They had missed him as well.

There's a fond sensation in being missed by those you hold in high regard.

Rose, Elizabeth, and Victoria were overjoyed to see him. Victoria and Elizabeth were no longer little girls. They'd grown so tall, he nearly toppled over when they rushed him with hugs and kisses and, "Where have you been?" and, "Are you back for good?"

In the flurry of excitement, Ethan looked around for the one person he most hoped to see. He spotted her at the edge of the grounds. She was dressed for work, and watched the ecstasy of her sisters and her mother with a calm indifference. When he raised his hand to wave at her, she turned away and walked past the line of shrubs and out of sight.

The bubble in Ethan's stomach deflated, but he wasn't allowed a moment to process, for Mr. Hartford appeared at the entrance of the grand house and playfully chided his wife and daughters for suffocating the poor boy. He was invited inside and into Mr. Hartford's study to go over the terms of his employment.

He did not see Allison for two days.

On the third day of Ethan's new employment, Allison finally appeared in the fields. She was dressed for work—though she still looked very smart and dignified. As he approached the supply cart alongside the other workers, he said brightly, "Hello, Allison."

"Good morning," she said, then brushed past him and said good morning to the other workers with the same polite indifference.

Ethan shook his head and retrieved a spade.

Throughout the day, Ethan kept Allison in the corner of his eye. He beamed inwardly at how Allison navigated the workers. She pitched in where needed, offered guidance at particular points, and distributed water occasionally. She avoided the rows where Ethan was working and never once looked in his direction. This distance allowed him to appreciate how she'd taken over the management of the estate. She was more than the daughter of the estate owner. She was in command in every way.

With each passing moment, his admiration grew, as well as his confusion as to why she was completely cold in his presence.

At the afternoon lunch break, he deliberately took his meal to where Allison sat on the back of a supply cart. He went around behind so she could not escape before she saw him. He was just sitting down next to her when she noticed him and very decidedly jumped off the cart.

"Allison," Ethan said.

She paused and lifted her chin.

"What is wrong?"

"What do you mean?"

He gestured to the space between them. "Are you angry with me?"

She lifted her chin higher. "Of course not."

Ethan narrowed his eyes. "You're sure?"

"Absolutely," she confirmed, though her eyes told a different story.

Before Ethan could challenge her further, she said in a low voice, "How can I be angry at someone I don't even know?"

Ethan's jaw dropped, and Allison sauntered away.

The following day Allison was no different, maintaining distance and never once looking in his direction. The cold barrier between them was so dense, Ethan felt he smacked into it at every turn.

This was not going to work, and he was desperate to discover what was making the woman he'd spent years dreaming of so completely hostile.

At four o'clock, Ethan concocted an excuse to return to the shed when he saw Allison walking in that direction. He met her at the door as she was exiting. She stopped suddenly when she saw him.

There was a small flicker of surprise and uncertainty just before she steeled her face again, but Ethan had just glimpsed her with her guard down, and it bolstered his courage enough to say, "This is a bit childish, don't you think?"

"To what are you referring?" she asked icily.

"Ignoring me. Treating me like I don't exist. Clearly something is wrong between us."

Allison glanced to the left. Her voice was flat when she said, "Yes, very childish. Almost as childish as disappearing without a word and leaving nothing but total silence for five. *Whole. Years.*" She spun on her heels and headed for the footbridge that crossed the brook.

Ethan followed (of course) and soon his heart was racing as they neared the bank of the brook where they'd spent nearly every Saturday night the summer he'd last seen her.

When they reached the place, she stopped, threw her hands in the air and cried, "*Why* did I come here?"

Ethan shoved his hands in his pockets. "This was our spot."

Allison rounded on him. "I *know* that, which is why I did not intend to come here." She began to march past him.

"Allison," he said desperately. "What did you mean, 'nothing but silence for five whole years'?"

Allison bunched her fists. "All that education and you're still so ignorant. How can you expect me to just behave as usual when you left without a word and never said anything for five years?"

"But I did—I did write you," Ethan pleaded.

"What?" Allison's fists dropped to her sides.

"I wrote every week."

"You wrote *me* every week?"

"No, not directly to you. I wrote your father. But I fully intended for you to read them. In fact, I didn't write a single letter without thinking of you."

Allison crossed her arms. "Did you tell my father to let me read them?"

"No, not specifically."

"Then *why* would my father give me his private correspondence with you?"

Ethan ran a hand through his dark hair. "I suppose he wouldn't have known. But I swear to you Allison, I never meant for you to hear nothing from me."

"Well I didn't."

"I can see that now." Ethan sidled over to a tree and leaned his shoulder against it. He sighed. "That took the wind out of our sails, didn't it?"

Allison's eyes glazed as she stared straight ahead. "I'm still angry, I just don't know who to be angry at."

"Be angry at me, I've got nothing else to lose."

"Don't pout, you were more at fault than I was."

"What's this? Allison Hartford admitting she's at fault?"

"Shove off. You're just as stubborn."

"Yes, but I've never claimed otherwise."

They both smiled tentatively, then silence like an oppressive fog settled over them. For the first time since returning home, Ethan feared he might lose Allison forever. So he did the only irrational thing he could think of to bring them back. "Do you still have the rope you used to climb out of your window with?"

he asked, forcing his old mischief into his words.

Allison's jaw tightened. "Why in the world would I still have that?"

Ethan pushed off the tree and took a few steps closer to her. "Don't tell me you never snuck out when I wasn't here?"

Just the smallest bit of sadness tinged Allison's voice when she said, "I never had another reason to."

It was only a little hope, but Ethan's heart soared upward in a short burst. "Might I entice you to use it tonight?"

"What for?"

"To meet me, of course."

Allison rolled her eyes, but he could tell she was putting in great effort to remain aloof. "We're not children anymore," she said.

Ethan grinned. As he stepped around her, he leaned close to her ear and whispered, "Exactly."

It was late and most of the family had retired for the evening. Allison remained fully clothed, and stood beside her bed, staring down at the rope she'd retrieved from the bottom of a drawer.

She chided herself for keeping it, the notion seeming so sentimental and childish when she had finally accepted she would never see Ethan again.

Just on time, Rose passed by Allison's slightly open door. She poked her head inside, witnessed Allison's attire and the rope on her bed, and said, "What is that for?"

Allison kept her eyes on the bed. "For climbing out the window."

Rose stepped into the room and shut the door. "Why are you climbing out the window?"

"I have not entirely decided I am going to."

Rose tiptoed closer and glanced at the rope. "Allison, what's going on? You've been out of sorts ever since Ethan returned. Has something happened?"

Allison sighed deeply and looked at her sister. Rose was not Samantha, but she was still a loyal friend. Allison allowed her to see the agony she was feeling. "He wants me to meet him tonight. The way we used to, every Saturday the summer before he left."

Rose's eyes widened so much they nearly consumed her face. "You used to sneak out and meet Ethan at night—alone?"

Allison nodded, both dreading and hoping for an astounded reprimand for her improper behavior.

What Rose did next was a complete surprise. She clapped her hands once and giggled. "Allison Hartford! How scandalous. But you are going, aren't you? You must!"

Allison hushed her. "Don't wake the whole house."

Rose giggled again. She went to the window and threw it open. "A young man awaits you. What are you still doing here?"

Allison squared off with her sister. "Rose, you are the most practical, polite person I know. If you tell me this is a bad idea, I will listen to you."

Rose smiled, and tossed one end of the rope out the window.

Ethan waited by the brook. He'd brought a blanket as he'd done a dozen times the fateful summer when he'd unexpectedly fallen in love with his childhood friend.

He felt her coming before he saw her. She walked slowly, covered in moonlight, and he thought she might be as nervous as he was.

And Allison was rarely nervous.

She didn't meet his eyes, but he smiled anyway. "I forgot how loud everything sounds when you're trying to be quiet," he said, referring to his own escape from his aunt's house.

Allison said nothing and sank down onto the blanket. Ethan desperately wanted to join her, to chatter away about inconsequential things the way they always had.

But Allison was right. They weren't children anymore, and he couldn't be naïve and think they'd go back to the way they'd been.

"There are some things to be said," Ethan began, remaining on his feet. "First, I should have apologized earlier about the letters. I didn't intend to abandon you, but you were abandoned nonetheless. I am sorry. I can't expect you to know how much I cared about you when all you knew was silence."

Allison lifted her head to peer at him. He crouched down so his features wouldn't be shadowed by the darkness. "I did care for you," he went on. "I told your father so, the day before I left. He wanted me to go to school, but I wanted to stay here forever. I tried to get him to let me, but my confession only made him more insistent that I receive my education first."

Allison's jaw tightened. "So my father forced you to go?"

"No, nothing like that. I mean, he was very convincing. I hated leaving, but I knew he was right."

"Ethan," Allison tilted her head. "May I ask, how did you pay for university?"

Ethan sat back on his heels. "You haven't figured that part out yet?"

"My father paid for your schooling?"

"Yes."

"Then did you return here out of obligation?"

Ethan shook his head adamantly. "Now that I've had plenty of time to think on it, I believe he wanted me to have choices. But I only ever wanted to work here."

"Why?"

"Because it's my home. I love the work of producing something from the ground. Of cultivating the earth. I love this place and I love your family. Besides, my aunt is all alone. We are each other's only family. I left her for a while, but I cannot leave her again."

Allison leaned forward, waiting for something more. But Ethan wasn't ready for that part yet. "I'm here because I want to be here," he said. "I am forever grateful and indebted to your father. He gave me the wide world and an invaluable education. But I'm here of my own free will."

Allison scrutinized him beneath the light of the moon. "You told my father you cared about me?"

"Yes."

"Just me? Not my sisters?"

"Yes."

Allison struggled over words until she finally said, "Then why did you leave without saying goodbye?"

Ethan sank forward onto his knees. "That is one part of my conduct I cannot defend. I believe my heart was broken and I couldn't bear to see you. I thought I might break into pieces."

At these words, a tear escaped its carefully concealed hiding place and slid down Allison's cheek. Her chin quivered, and she whispered, "But what about *my* broken heart?"

Until that moment, Ethan and Allison had yet to even shake hands. The distance between them was a gulf of unanswered questions and years not knowing what the other was thinking.

In that moment, watching the pain of five years revealed as Allison's lower lip quivered and she rocked a little while hugging her knees, he crossed the gulf and took one of her hands. He waited until she looked at him before he said, "There's one more thing. Something I believe I didn't even understand until today. I could have written to you, but—well, I wanted you to have choices, too. I waited and waited to hear of you getting married. When news of it never came, I returned with no small amount of hope. Perhaps— perhaps you were waiting for me, too? I can see now how foolish that was. I can't promise I'm much wiser now, but I do know I never stopped loving you. Not for one moment."

With these words, the walls were shattered. Neither

of them could remember who kissed who first (perhaps they both had the idea at the same time). Either way, their lips connected, and Ethan's arms circled around her as she slid her hands along his back and gripped his shirt, pulling him closer.

Ethan sighed as his mouth moved over hers, the longing to hold her finally satisfied.

At long last, they were together, and nothing would ever separate them again.

8

To Test the Mettle of the Man

The evening had descended and Mr. Hartford was in his study with his feet propped up and a book in his hands. He was just settling in, when Allison appeared in the doorway, hands on hips and a determined set of her chin.

He nearly dropped his book.

"Father, I have a score to settle with you," she said.

"What have I done now?"

"Ethan wrote to you, every week, for five years, and you never shared those letters with me?"

Mr. Hartford's gray eyebrows slid upward on his forehead. "Was I supposed to?"

"Yes!" Allison strode forward and placed her fists on her father's desk. "He was our brother and he just up and left. Did you not think we'd want to know what happened to him?"

Mr. Hartford's eyebrows slid downward. "Come to think of it, he did share quite a lot of detail. I often thought he might have forgotten he was writing to me. But then, Loretta Humphrey did say he was lonely..."

"Lonely! Father, why did you not tell us this? We were his sisters. We could have all written to him. And Letty said nothing, either?"

Mr. Hartford stood and rounded his desk to face his daughter. He chewed the edge of his spectacles as he weighed his next words. "My dear, before he left, Ethan revealed to me he cared deeply for you. We thought it best he go away for a little while—see the world, receive an education. However, I counseled this, thinking you were unaware of his feelings for you. Indeed, you might not recall, but after I received his first letter, I made mention of his welfare and—well—you were very angry."

Allison felt the blood drain from her cheeks. Of course she remembered it. She'd snapped at her father, saying she didn't care a jot about what happened to Ethan and had fled outdoors to be away from any thoughts of him. However, there was not a single spot on the estate that did not contain a memory with Ethan, and she'd returned to the house very sad.

Was *that* why her father had neglected to bring him up?

Mr. Hartford stepped closer. "Did I—did I perhaps misread your feelings? Did you—return his affection?"

Allison leaned back against the desk. "Yes. I believe I did."

"Then I am sorry," said Mr. Hartford. "Had I known, I would have taken better care."

Allison sighed. "I have been so angry with him for

so long. Can it be this was all a result of a dreadful misunderstanding?"

Mr. Hartford took his daughter's hand. "It would seem so. Though I had my own role to play. I do hope you will forgive me." It was clear to him, sometimes it was easier to be angry at someone than admit you loved them.

Allison shrugged one shoulder. "I wish to see the letters, since he intended for me to read them."

"Of course." Mr. Hartford retrieved the letters from a cabinet across the room. He handed her a box of them (five years of weekly letters amounted to a very full box).

"Thank you," Allison mumbled, and approached the door. When she reached it, she turned back. "Father, when Ethan calls on you this evening to ask for my hand, I do hope you will say yes."

Mr. Hartford blinked rapidly several times. "Does he intend to propose, then?"

Allison nodded. "He already has." She departed with as much gusto as she'd entered.

A heavenly glow from the morning sun followed Ethan and Allison down Main Street. Never ones to uphold propriety, they walked hand in hand, oblivious to the wide-eyed stares of their Tree Town neighbors. It wasn't an intentional defiance of the hidden rules of society, rather the years apart made them quite unconscious of anything other than the sheer bliss of being in one another's company.

One of the town gawkers was Daniel Copeland, who had, for a fraction of a moment, a sudden burst of deep concern inside his chest. He stared openly at the couple until he felt sure they must—indeed—be engaged. He then crammed his hat further down on his head and ducked under the shade of an awning.

Not five seconds after Ethan rapped on the door of Samantha and William's house did the door swing open, revealing Samantha. She stared back and forth between Allison and Ethan. When she saw their beaming faces and interlocked hands, she broke into a wide grin, squealed, and embraced Allison. She hopped up and down—blocking the doorway should the two guests have wanted to enter.

William appeared behind Samantha and gently made way for Allison and Ethan. He closed the door behind them all, shutting out many disappointed onlookers.

Once inside the safety of the house, Allison and Samantha squeezed each other, and William shook hands with Ethan. Then they switched places, and Samantha embraced her new brother while William kissed Allison on the cheek.

William offered Allison and Ethan the sofa, and he and Samantha sat in the separate armchairs. Samantha danced in her seat. "We haven't seen either of you in several days and were so worried something had gone horribly wrong. What a surprise to see you both here—together!"

"A surprise indeed," William added. He turned his head to wink privately at his wife.

"No one is more surprised than I am." Allison

settled against Ethan as his arm draped about her shoulders. "A week ago, I did not think I'd ever see him again."

"A week ago, I had grand plans of sweeping her off her feet," said Ethan. "I'm very lucky she didn't send me back whence I came."

"Tell us everything." Samantha clasped her hands in her lap to keep from flapping them about in ecstasy.

Ethan and Allison poured out the entire tale— complete with every twist and turn of misunderstandings and assumed motives.

"I knew there was more to the story," Samantha crowed.

"Still, it could have turned out poorly." Ethan winced slightly.

Allison took Ethan's hand and looked at him. "We are together now," she consoled. "And we'll never separate again."

They became so lost in one another's eyes that William had to draw them back to the conversation with a subtle clearing of his throat.

"Shall we to church?" Samantha asked.

"Must we?" Allison groaned.

"I think the town will find out sooner or later," said William. He stood and offered Samantha his hand. "It'll be nice to have all the attention elsewhere."

"Let them stare and have their gossip," said Ethan. "It'll not dampen our joy."

"You've been away too long," Allison chided. "Tree Town is merciless."

"They used to whisper foreboding prospects that

all the Hartford sisters would die spinsters," said Samantha. "The tune is likely to change now."

"Until they find some other fault," Allison mused, but she smiled brightly all the way to Sunday service.

Ethan and Allison received many stares from the congregation when they entered together. As they found the Hartford family pew, Samantha leaned upward to whisper in her husband's ear, "One victory, three more to go."

William smiled and squeezed his wife's hand.

At that moment, nothing seemed impossible.

Ethan and Allison's story is not yet complete. That same afternoon, they wandered to the untouched hill where the sisters usually spent their Saturday evenings. Together, the new couple watched as the sun began to set on the most tumultuous week of either of their lives.

While the warmth of their happiness consumed them both, there was one thing Allison still worried over. But her concern would not ease, so she broached the subject with her intended.

Never one for delicate interludes, she began, "You know the law states when a woman marries, any property she owns becomes the property of her husband."

Ethan inclined his head, waiting.

Allison kept her eyes on the sinking sun. "There is one way around it, I've discovered. A husband must sign a document, relinquishing all rights to the property—basically, he must bequeath it to his wife as if he had already died. Though still some legal cases favor the husbands, even with this document."

Ethan remained very still, and Allison was afraid to look at him.

"I've long said I would never marry," Allison pressed onward. "My father has no sons, and I never wanted to see all of his labor—and the labor of my sisters—entailed away to strange men who do not value the land as we do. If I were to remain unmarried, then there would always be a Hartford at the helm of the estate. Of course, this would involve my father leaving only money to my other sisters, but should they marry, they would have no need of the estate."

Allison finally turned to face Ethan. "We all love our home, but I love it most of all my sisters. I know you love it, too, but surely you must see how cruel an injustice it would be for you to inherit my father's estate upon his death, simply because you are a man and married to one of his daughters?"

Ethan's mouth hitched up, pondering Allison's words. He watched the anxiety shudder over her features, and for the first time he questioned the methods of his soon-to-be father-in-law. He drew Allison closer and said, "You need not worry, my love, as your father has already taken care of this dishonorable detail."

Allison drew back. "What do you mean?"

"I suppose it's to test the mettle of the man intent on marrying one of his daughters. He told me last night he would only give me permission to marry you if I relinquished all rights to the estate once we were man and wife. However, this also involves you naming me your heir, should you die before I do. It's all very confusing, but of course I agreed."

Allison blinked twice. "My father knew about this? Why did he not say anything?"

"He told me I should tell no one, as he didn't wish the word getting about the countryside he was attempting to defy the law—it might cause trouble. It's a cruel world, and he feared the repercussions would fall upon your heads—as it always seems to— even though he takes pains to shield you and your sisters from it."

Allison's eyes widened. "Why does my father always do these things in secret?"

Ethan shrugged one shoulder. "I supposed he wished to carry the burden himself. Though he certainly underestimated your ability to find a loophole on your own."

"Then you don't mind?"

"I was a penniless orphan to begin with. Of course I don't mind having a rich wife."

"Be serious. You don't mind giving away your claims, though the law favors you, as a man?"

Ethan rested his forehead against Allison's. He held her gaze for a long moment before he said, "All I want is you."

As the sun finished its plunge beneath the horizon, Allison drew Ethan's lips to her own, kissing him deeply to the backdrop of a purple and golden sky.

She never ceased to wonder at how one's fate could change so suddenly.

Nor did she ever doubt her choice of husband.

9

I Do Hope Dessert is Good

Allison and Ethan would always remember the heroic part Rose played in encouraging Allison to resolve her differences with Ethan. Though Rose never regretted the hand she played in her sister's happiness, not many days after Allison and Ethan's engagement, she found herself amidst a torrent of conflicting emotions, torn between the joy she felt for her sister and the disappointment she felt for herself.

Soon she would be parted from not one, but two of her closest sisters. And though her family was determined the women of the household should have an occupation and not merely bide their time for marriage, she was aware she had no prospects and felt the cruel fate of spinsterhood closing in around her (at twenty-three, nearly all her friends had already married).

With these thoughts and feelings swimming and swirling inside her person, Rose was in desperate need of a distraction.

Her older sister and brother-in-law were happy to oblige.

William was needed in Port Town once again, and Samantha resolved to go with him, taking Rose as her companion.

On their second day in town, Rose and Samantha received an invitation to luncheon at the home of one of their friends, a Mrs. Hammerson. Mrs. Hammerson was a pinnacle of society and the first married among the crop of young women at the coast. Her marriage catapulted several other girls into marriage, and all of these women were invited.

Samantha was the newest bride. Therefore, she was petted and praised and congratulated. The Temples were not unknown by the community at the coast and William had been a mysterious bachelor for years on end. That he should marry a Hartford was strange indeed, but the marriage itself was enough to absolve Samantha of any crime in that regard.

As the women sipped their tea and nibbled their scones, Mrs. Hammerson said, "Did we hear correctly Allison Hartford is engaged?"

Samantha smiled. "She is. To a young man we all know and love. We could not be happier."

A Mrs. Smythe raised her teacup to her lips and looked very much as if she were repressing a sneer. "He is a farmhand, is he not?"

Samantha nodded. An awkward silence followed.

Mrs. Hammerson laughed to ease the tension. "Well, we all know the Hartfords have strange ways. But they are happy. Let us toast to happiness, even if it is not conventional." The gathered women joined her in raising their cups.

Samantha glanced sideways at Rose, who pretended the toast was not taking place.

"When is your turn coming?" said Mrs. Smythe to Rose. "I thought for sure you'd make a match before Allison. I'm surprised Allison is to be married at all, but her choice certainly suites her." She laughed in a way that invited the other women to join her. They acquiesced, and Samantha slipped her hand into Rose's to squeeze it for consolation.

During their walk home, Samantha made the decision not to accept any more invitations for the duration of their stay, for Rose's sake.

Between dining in the boarding house; shopping for hats, gloves, and material; and walks up and down the sand dunes on the beach, Samantha kept Rose occupied.

On the fourth day of their stay, Samantha awoke with a headache. Since Rose had expressed upon first arriving that she would like to ride, Samantha (not being fond of horses) suggested Rose rent a horse, take her pencils and paints, and a basket lunch, and make a day of it.

It was a remarkably fine day, with clouds masking the sun, creating the most beautiful lighting for Rose's sketch pad and pencils. However, she soon found she did not like to be alone. With no one to talk to, her mind wandered into places she did not like it to go. She forced herself to concentrate on her sketch of the shoreline.

In her earnestness to control her thoughts, she did not notice the beginnings of a gale until large droplets of rain began to hit and smudge her pallet.

Drawing her eyes away from her sketch, she noticed how dark the sky had become, how rough the sea was, and how cold she felt—her summer wrap providing very little protection. Quickly, she gathered up her things and tried to steady the uneasy horse while loading her effects.

The wind kicked up the sand and the rain poured. By the time she mounted, Rose was drenched and could barely see through the rain as it pelted her face. No sooner had she begun to urge the animal forward, then lightning flashed across the sky, chased by a deafening crack of thunder.

The horse reared, and in an instant, she was lying face down in the wet sand. When she looked up, the horse was gone.

There was nothing to do but walk toward town, which was a good two miles away. Hugging herself and shivering, one step at a time, she set forth. Her own misery so consumed her, she had no thought for how worried the others at the boarding house would be.

Samantha was beside herself. She had noticed the storm forming in the sky and hoped Rose had enough sense to come home before it began. When the rain began to fall (a steady drizzle at first but soon turned to downpour) she paced back and forth in the front parlor of the boarding house, praying her sister was not injured or taken ill. Every few minutes, she'd glance out the window, hoping to see Rose.

William arrived an hour or so after the downpour had begun. He entered the boarding house bringing with him a certain Reuben Dudley (with whom we are already acquainted).

"Look here, Samantha," said William. "I've brought someone to join our party for supper." He shook out his umbrella (he was familiar with the unpredictable weather and always carried it with him). His coat was still saturated, though, as the wind had attacked the umbrella. He and Reuben began to remove their drenched hats and coats.

Samantha rushed to William and took hold of his coat mid-removal. "Rose has been gone all day. She's out there caught in this storm. I just know something terrible has happened."

William's eyes widened, and he shrugged back into his coat.

Reuben looked between Samantha and William. "Rose Hartford is in town?" he asked.

William ignored him. "Don't worry, darling," he said to Samantha. "I'm sure she's waiting at the stables for the rain to stop. I'll go there at once and bring her home."

This William did, only to return a half hour later to report Rose was not there. He hesitated and shifted his gaze to Reuben.

"What is it?" Samantha demanded.

"The horse returned over an hour ago."

Samantha barely had time to let this information sink in before Reuben suggested he use his own horse to go in search of Rose.

"I'll go with you," said William, replacing his soaked hat atop his head.

Reuben held up a hand. "There's no need for both of us to be out in this. Stay with your wife in case her sister comes home." He turned to Samantha. "Would you mind telling me where she was going?"

Samantha stammered a response, and Reuben left.

As they waited, Samantha instructed the boarding house staff to prepare a bath for Rose. She had tea brought in, but it grew cold, as she and William were far too preoccupied to drink it.

"I should have gone with Reuben," said William, swinging his hat between his knees as he sat on the sofa.

"Darling, you should change. Your clothes were soaked through," said Samantha.

"I might be needed again. Besides, the fire has dried them out."

Samantha sat beside him and rested an elbow on the armrest, with her chin on her fist. As the minutes dragged on, she began to worry something truly dreadful had happened to her sister.

Finally, the anxious couple heard the door to the boarding house bang open and Reuben's voice saying, "We're back, and she's all right."

Samantha and William rushed to the front door. William took the shivering Rose out of Reuben's protective arms and escorted her to a seat near the fireplace. Samantha draped a blanket over Rose's legs and a shawl around her thin shoulders. She then turned to the curious house staff who lingered in the doorway, advising them to heat up the water in the bath.

In the bustle to make Rose comfortable, Reuben was forgotten. As he stood dripping on the threshold of the door, he assumed the supper invitation was postponed. He shuffled his feet, wondering if he should say goodbye or simply depart without interrupting the ministrations over poor Rose, whose lips were blue from cold.

Shoving his hat down over his ears, he made ready to leave, but before he could get out the door, Samantha noticed him and said, "I insist you join us for supper. It is the very least we can do after your heroic deed."

Reuben hesitated.

William looked up from where he was pouring tea for Rose. "How about we reschedule for tomorrow evening? Reuben is drenched and exhausted, and Rose needs her rest."

Reuben nodded. "A fine idea. I'll be off, then." He retreated out the door before Samantha could protest.

Samantha placed her hands on her hips. "William, he just spent over an hour in the rain looking for my sister. We could have at least offered him a hot meal?"

As William leaned down to hand Rose her tea, he tilted his head in her direction and raised his eyes at Samantha.

Samantha looked at Rose, saw how pitiful she was, with wet hair plastered around her face, blue lips, and a nose that was beginning to turn red. It suddenly occurred to her why Reuben had been invited in the first place, and she couldn't restrain the grin that spread across her face.

Luckily, Rose was shivering so much (she'd gone through quite a shock), that she didn't notice the silent communication between the husband and wife.

Samantha threw herself onto the couch beside Rose and begged to know what had happened.

"I don't really know," said Rose. "All of a sudden it was raining. Then the horse threw me. I seemed to have been walking for hours. I thought I'd never reach town. Just when I was about to despair, I saw Mr. Dudley coming on his horse."

Samantha smiled. "It was very kind of him to rescue you."

Rose squinted at the fireplace. "He didn't say a word, just threw me onto the back of his horse and headed for home." She hugged the shawl more tightly around her shoulders. "You shouldn't have made him come for me."

"We didn't make him, he insisted," said Samantha.

"I would have been fine," said Rose.

"You said you were about to despair."

"Even so..." said Rose. Then she gasped, "My horse! I have lost him. What will I do?"

"Don't worry," said William. "He's already returned to the stables."

Rose sagged with relief.

Samantha stood. "Shall we get you upstairs and into a bath?"

Rose slept late the next morning. She did not at all seem interested that Reuben was coming to supper, nor did she seem grateful for her rescue.

In the afternoon, as she rested in the parlor with a book, Samantha asked, "Why was it so upsetting for Reuben to come for you? He was only being kind."

"I don't even know him," said Rose. "A complete stranger threw me onto his horse without a single word. It was mortifying."

"You spent two weeks with him."

"Two weeks in which he barely spoke a word. Why couldn't William have come for me?"

"Reuben wanted to come."

Rose shoved her nose further into her book, making it clear she did not want to continue the conversation.

Samantha wished she could send a message to William before he arrived, warning him of Rose's sour mood.

The supper with Reuben would likely be a disaster.

That evening, Rose's spirits remained dampened. She came to supper late, nodded to Reuben when he rose to greet her, but she said nothing.

Reuben had never been a great talker, but his lack of conversational ease had never been an issue when he had dined with Samantha and William in the past. Samantha was usually witty and sociable and William could carry on his end with little effort.

But on this night, William was not in an entertaining mood. Blame it on the weather, if you will, but he was quite glum and slightly preoccupied.

You can imagine how poor Samantha felt. She was in good spirits, but no one in the party was catering to her mood. She wanted to help Rose and Reuben become acquainted, but they both refused to look at one another, being more interested in the food on their plates. The shallow questions she asked did nothing to incite conversation. Soon, she also fell to silence and found her food more interesting than the dinner party.

They were a sad lot, and were in desperate need of a jolting of some sort. Fate waited for the opportune moment, then sent an enormous rat running through the dining hall. Many patrons, including Samantha and Rose, jumped onto their chairs.

Once the initial fright was over, the sisters began to laugh at the red-faced chef who was chasing the rat with a pot (though it was unclear what he intended to do with it). Reuben and William joined in the chase and with the use of chairs, and strategically placed boot-clad feet, the rat was goaded out into the front hall, and then out the front door.

When Reuben and William reentered the dining hall, the boarders applauded. The two friends smiled and parted the way for the chef, who took an elaborate bow before he scurried back to the kitchen to help prepare the next course.

The scuffle had been exactly what they needed to liven them up. Rose and Samantha entertained them all with childhood stories of rats they had chased in the kitchen at home on the estate. It was very inappropriate conversation for supper, but at least it was conversation.

Nearing the last course, Rose sighed and leaned back in her chair. "I do hope dessert is good." She placed her fork delicately on her plate. "I'm going to need something sweet after that excitement."

"I'm sorry to disappoint you," said Reuben, voice neutral. "But I'm afraid dessert just went out the front door."

For the first time that evening, Rose looked Reuben in the eyes. There was a brief, pregnant pause, then Rose threw back her head and laughed.

Samantha and William glanced at one another. Slow smiles crept across their faces. Beneath the table, William reached to take Samantha's hand, acknowledging what they had both just witnessed.

Lightning had struck.

10

Enjoy Your Ride

August was closing in on September, and everyone in the town hoped the hot days were coming to an end. That day, it was quite warm, and Daniel Copeland was in a cheerful mood when he returned home after a day sauntering about Tree Town.

The marble floors of the grand house echoed with the sound of Daniel's footsteps. Soon the entire house echoed with his voice. "Mother!" he shouted. "Mother, where are you?"

"I'm in here," Mrs. Copeland's voice came from one of the several sitting rooms lining the foyer.

Daniel entered and threw his hat upon a sofa and threw his gangly form onto another. "Do you think our land could turn any profit?" he asked.

The graying, rigid figure of Mrs. Copeland ceased its embroidery.

She turned toward Daniel and lowered her spectacles. "Whatever do you mean?" she asked slowly.

"We have so much of it. Do you think we could farm it?"

There was a dreadful pause. Mrs. Copeland was sure this was another one of her son's fanciful visions upon which he seldom followed through. She replied with, "Your father—God rest him—loved the land the way it is. I would hate to change it."

Daniel sat forward. "We don't have to change all of it. We could keep the large wooded parts for hunting, like always. We could use only a few of the fields for farming. Like the Hartfords do."

At the mention of the Hartfords, Mrs. Copeland's eyes widened. She began stitching furiously. "The Hartfords are of the working class," she said. "We have no need of turning a profit with the land. The idea is ridiculous."

"Acres and acres of land are just sitting around. It wouldn't hurt to use it for *something*."

Mrs. Copeland sniffed, and her chin quivered. "No, Daniel. I said no. I don't want to discuss it again."

"Can we at least sell some of it?"

Daniel leaned forward earnestly as Mrs. Copeland gasped.

"Or rent it out. Have tenants. There are plenty of people looking for land to settle. If we aren't going to use it, we might as well let someone else. It's perfectly logical."

As Daniel watched the color drain from Mrs. Copeland's face, he thought perhaps he should have begun with the option of selling it and then broached the idea of farming. It might have made the idea of working it themselves more palatable. As it were, he had known his mother would say no before he even asked the question.

Mrs. Copeland exaggerated the effort it took to control the emotion in her voice. "Why would you think of changing things from the way your father left them? He said nothing to me about farming it or selling it. He loved it the way it is. Please don't speak of this again." She used the edge of her embroidery to wipe at her eyes (though there were no actual tears present).

Daniel rested his elbows on his knees and tried to get his mother to look at him. "I don't want to upset you, Mother. Perhaps it's just a bad time."

"I will never sell the land," Mrs. Copeland said without flinching. "If you love me, you will never raise this subject again."

Daniel got up and went to the sofa where his mother was seated. He took her hand. "I do love you," he said. "I only want you to be happy. I just thought you'd be happy seeing me busy with something."

Mrs. Copeland pulled her hand away from her son and silently returned to stitching.

Daniel heaved his body up to standing and made his way to the door.

"You left your hat," Mrs. Copeland called after him.

Daniel went back for it. He looked at his mother when he retrieved it, but she refused to meet his eyes.

Daniel marched outside, going nowhere of consequence. After a long walk through fields, woods, and over streams, he found himself at the stables. They were mostly empty, except for two coach horses and his own black stallion.

His horse had cost a small fortune, but he had goaded his mother into purchasing it. He had wanted to buy it when he pictured himself riding through town, the envy of everyone who saw him.

As he grew older, the amusement he got from the stares died down. He now rode only for pleasure, and only where no one could see him. He rode fast, too. Sometimes he hoped he would ride so fast the horse would throw him and he would be finished with his bleak life. But when he remembered he would leave his mother all alone in the world, he became more cautious.

After he'd saddled the horse and rode out of sight of the house, he allowed it to roam wherever it pleased and at whatever pace it wished.

The Copeland estate stretched for miles along the east side of the county. It bordered the main road almost to the edge of town. In a lonely field, separated from the road by a sturdy fence, the horse decided to stop for a rest.

The very expensive horse was often as unruly and unpredictable as its master. Without warning, it sank to its knees. Daniel was fortunate enough to have leapt to safety before the horse began to roll. The horse, perturbed that its frolicking was inhibited by a stately saddle, got up in irritation and stood looking at Daniel, who sat sulking in the grass.

Laughter from the direction of the road startled Daniel, and he glanced over his shoulder. He rolled his eyes and began to get up when he saw Victoria and Elizabeth Hartford. Victoria was standing on a rail of the fence and was watching the horse with fascination.

Daniel felt no obligation to speak to the Hartford girls. They were from a family that brought him nothing but irritation. He grasped the bridle of his horse, but he could still feel their eyes watching him.

He turned around once more. They were still standing and staring, but Elizabeth was tugging on Victoria's arm, trying to get her to leave.

"What are you looking at?" Daniel demanded.

"Looking at you," said Victoria. "It's a beautiful horse."

"Yes, I know," said Daniel.

"May I pet him?" Victoria asked.

"Victoria!" Elizabeth hissed under her breath, but Daniel heard her.

If only to perturb the older sister, Daniel walked determinedly toward the fence, leading the noble steed behind him.

Elizabeth waited for Victoria to pet the horse with arms crossed and a smug look on her face.

Daniel found he enjoyed her irritation immensely.

"What's his name?" asked Victoria.

"Uh—Ebony." Daniel watched with curiosity the sparkling joy that consumed Victoria's face as she stroked the horse's neck.

Elizabeth interrupted the silence by saying, "We must go, Victoria."

Victoria smiled at Daniel. "Thank you, Daniel. I hope you enjoy your ride. Goodbye, Ebony." Victoria gave the horse a final pat on the neck.

Daniel shook his head and remounted the horse, thinking it silly that petting a horse could make Victoria so happy.

During his ride back to the stables, Daniel had a thought. It was a very wicked thought, but the pleasure of it began to bubble in his stomach, making its way all the way up through his chest. A scheme for diverting the younger Hartford sisters was well formed by the time he reached the stables.

He surrendered Ebony to a groom, saying, "Thank you, Andrews," and began walking toward the main house.

The groom stared after him with mouth wide.

He'd never in his life heard Mr. Copeland say "thank you" to anyone.

"I wish you wouldn't be so informal with Daniel Copeland." Elizabeth tugged on Victoria's arm as they headed for Tree Town.

"Why not? It's just Daniel..." Victoria allowed herself to be led by her older sister, knowing better than to protest too much.

"Exactly!" Elizabeth exclaimed.

"What's so bad about Daniel?"

"Oh, I don't know, maybe he's done nothing but criticize and mock our family since the day we were born."

"I don't know that it's that bad..."

"Yes, it is," Elizabeth stated. She could still remember soundly the day she showed up at Sunday service in a new dress. She was very proud of the dress and enjoyed the compliments paid to her by the Tree Town residents.

Then, out of nowhere, Daniel had appeared at her side, whispering, "Putting on airs, are we? I thought the Hartfords were above such things."

Elizabeth had instantly deflated and every bit of enjoyment evaporated.

She did not like Daniel Copeland.

The two sisters trudged along. Elizabeth was still pulling Victoria, though many minutes had passed and she was no longer sure why. It wasn't like Victoria was going to escape and run back to Daniel. It had just been a simple pat on the horse's sleek neck.

But Victoria had been cordial to their greatest critic and Elizabeth would have preferred she behave otherwise.

Elizabeth slowed, and Victoria chanced another question. "Why do you think Daniel acts the way he does?"

Ah, so Victoria did see it. Elizabeth made a "humph" sound. She was worried Victoria's naivety was going to get her into trouble. "Isn't it obvious?" she said. "He's *jealous*. We're happy and he's miserable. It's as simple as that."

Victoria was silent just a moment before saying, "Oh, I don't know if it's *that* simple," very quietly.

They reached the grocers. Typically Elizabeth dragged one of her sisters along with her to visit Mr. Cole's mother. Since Rose and Samantha were at the coast and Allison was usually busy managing the estate, Victoria was her only option.

"Hello, Mr. Cole." Victoria went to the counter where Mr. Cole was going over account books, but had looked up the moment the two young women had entered. He was bleary-eyed, and his face looked weary. (Elizabeth thought he seemed bleary-eyed and weary a lot these days.)

Mr. Cole smiled, and his smile shifted Elizabeth's mood. "Mr. Cole, we're here to see your mother," she said sweetly.

Mr. Cole transferred his gray eyes to hers. "I knew the first of the month was approaching. She always relaxes more and experiences a lift in spirits when she knows you'll be coming."

Elizabeth's insides rippled with pleasure. "What a lovely thing to say."

They all stood for a moment, not saying anything. Then Victoria cleared her throat (very loudly).

"Right," said Elizabeth. "You must have a lot of work to do. We'll be off then." Taking charge again, she yanked on Victoria's arm (for nothing better to do) and the two sisters ascended the back stairs to the Cole family apartment.

After their visit, Mr. Cole had finished his accounts and was in the midst of placing an order, but he set down his pen as the sisters neared the counter. "What were we reading today?" he asked.

"John Killner," Elizabeth responded, delighted that her taste was so sophisticated.

"Ah, the romantic poet." Mr. Cole leaned forward and placed his forearms on the counter. His sleeves were rolled up (as they usually were) and Elizabeth could see the muscles flexing above his wrists (even though she was keeping her eyes very focused on his face). The sight made her stomach to do an odd dance. She swallowed, noticing her mouth had gone inexplicably dry.

"Have you read much Killner lately?" Elizabeth inquired.

Mr. Cole shook his head. "Not much time for it I'm afraid."

Elizabeth inwardly berated herself. Of course he didn't have time to read. He was positively overwhelmed with the care of his mother and the store.

"I find him boring," said Victoria. "He says in fifteen stanzas what could have been said in five."

Mr. Cole chuckled. "A poet's prerogative, I'm sure."

"Well your mother enjoyed it," Elizabeth said curtly. She cut a look at Victoria, silently telling her not to mention that Mrs. Cole had done nothing but sit silently, staring into nothingness, and had given very little indication she even knew the sisters were in the room. "But I'm sure you have much work to do this afternoon. We'll leave you to it..." She extended her hand toward Victoria's arm, but Victoria skillfully danced out of reach.

Victoria said, "Goodbye Mr. Cole. See you at Sunday service."

Mr. Cole waved farewell as both sisters shoved through the door out onto the street.

"Mr. Cole was very quiet today," Victoria said, as they meandered toward home.

"Yes, he's usually much more lively. I suppose he's worried about his mother."

"She didn't seem any different to me."

"She wouldn't. You don't see her every month. I do. She's gotten progressively worse this past year." Elizabeth increased her pace, and Victoria trotted to keep up with her. "Mrs. Cole is very ill," Elizabeth continued. "And Mr. Cole is burdened with many responsibilities. It's why we must do our Christian duty and keep them company."

Victoria gave an exaggerated sigh. "We *know.* You remind us *every* month."

Elizabeth straightened her back and walked even faster.

Because something about Victoria's words pricked Elizabeth's conscience, making her wonder if her motives were not quite as unselfish as she thought they were.

11

They Think They Are Very Clever

The day after the timely storm, when the flicker of a small flame began inside two hearts, Rose was also struck with a terrible cold. This was not altogether unfortunate, for the rain continued to stop and start in spurts, and Rose was obliged to stay indoors for several days, anyway.

To fan the flame, each day around noon, William returned to the boarding house to take his meal with Samantha. Reuben was invited as well (and he nearly always accepted the invitation).

Due to her cold, Rose's nose was perpetually red, so just before noon, she would do the difficult work of powdering it. The powder was always wiped away with a handkerchief before the meal was half-way complete. She was quite tired, but always made an effort to join them for lunch.

This, Samantha and William saw as further sign of affection.

When the gloomy weather faded, Rose's cold also

abated. On the weekend, the small family decided to take their afternoon meal on the beach. Reuben again joined them, and they were all in high spirits as the sun bore down on them from the sky.

The hired man set up the picnic in a cove shaded by the cliffs. While they waited, William suggested a stroll. As they walked along the water's edge, Samantha and William picked up speed, leaving the would-be lovers quite behind. Considering Rose's recent recovery from her cold, they trusted she'd not try to catch up. Reuben was too much of a gentleman to let her walk alone.

Samantha and William disappeared around a cliff while Rose and Reuben meandered along, neither one of them speaking. The crashing waves provided a comfortable background noise, and Rose felt relaxed and refreshed. It was good to be outdoors after convalescing for a week, and Reuben had grown into an easy companion.

But Samantha and William's abrupt disappearance confirmed something she already suspected. She glanced at Reuben as he walked by her side, keeping his eyes on the moist sand. "You know what my brother and sister are up to, don't you?" she said.

Reuben looked ahead to where Samantha and William were no longer visible. "What are they up to?"

Rose adjusted her parasol, shifting it from one shoulder to the other. "They're trying to throw us together. I wasn't sure at first, but this little stunt absolutely confirms it."

Reuben raised his eyebrows, but kept his eyes focused forward.

"Tell me you didn't notice," Rose goaded.

Reuben shook his head. "I thought they might have invited me to Tree Town for such an occasion, but until today, I thought they'd given up."

Rose chuckled. "They think they're very clever. But we see through their schemes, don't we?"

Finally, Reuben looked at Rose. His eyes were warm and brown, and the little lines at their edges deepened when he smiled.

He wasn't a somber person, but he didn't smile often. When he did, Rose found she liked it quite a lot.

"They seem very happy together," Reuben said. "It's only natural they would want the same for their friends."

"Yes, only natural," Rose responded.

They walked on in silence before deciding to return to the picnic.

"Do you have siblings, Mr. Dudley?" Rose posed her parasol so she could see him clearly as he rested back on his elbows, legs kicked out in front of him. More casual than he'd ever been in her presence.

"I have three sisters. And please, call me Reuben."

"Three sisters? Older or younger?"

"One older. Two younger."

The picnic was spread out between them, and Rose picked up a slice of cold meat and began to nibble. "Our neighbor Ethan was the closest thing we had to a brother. Did you miss not having a brother?"

Reuben stared out at the ocean as he pondered her question. "I can't recall. I suppose I had plenty of friends at school and didn't feel the lack."

"And your sisters? Are you close with them?"

"Not as close as you are with your sisters. The youngest, Hannah, she is the closest. She never forgets to write."

"And do you ever forget to write to her?"

"Never," he answered. "I write her every week."

Rose raised her eyebrows. They were very close indeed.

Samantha and William took a considerably long time to arrive. When they did, Samantha threw herself onto the blanket beside Rose. "I'm famished," she exclaimed.

Rose couldn't resist. "That was rather a long walk to take just before lunch."

"We were having such a delightful time. Had it not been for our stomachs, we might have gone on for hours."

"You two should really explore the cliffs on the other side of the cove," said William. "We'll have plenty of daylight once we've finished eating."

"I think I might have myself a little nap after lunch." Samantha lay her head on Rose's shoulder.

"You don't mind staying a little longer, do you Reub?" William poured himself a glass of summer wine.

Reuben held out his own glass to William. "It's a lovely day," he said, another soft smile playing at his lips. "I don't mind at all."

From behind Rose's back, Samantha winked at her husband.

Two days following the picnic, William returned to the boarding house, whistling merrily. Samantha was lounging in their rooms, and glanced over the top of her book at her husband, as he began to change for supper. His whistling continued, as he swapped his business cravat for the dining cravat and kept peeking at Samantha in the mirror.

Samantha closed her book. "What on earth has got you so excited?" she asked.

William swiveled around. "I've got some news, but you have to promise not to say anything to Rose."

Samantha tossed her book and squealed. "Reuben is going to propose!"

William shook his head and held up one hand. "No, not yet."

Samantha slumped. "What can he be waiting for? They are clearly very fond of one another."

William grinned. "I said 'not yet' but I didn't say never. I happen to know two letters were dispatched today to your father and mother."

Samantha squealed again. "To ask their permission to marry her?"

William crossed to the settee and took a seat next to his wife. "To ask permission to begin a courtship."

"Why?" Samantha moaned. "What need have they of courting? They're both quite grown up and can surely know their own hearts and minds." Then she straightened abruptly. "But *Reuben* wrote two letters? How do you know? Did he tell you?"

"I was getting to that part," said William. "I asked him this morning how he felt about Rose."

"You did what?"

"He expressed his interest, and I advised entering your parents' good graces as quickly as possible. They've already met him, but I dispatched my own letter, recommending him as an appropriate match. We have nothing to do now, but wait."

Samantha blinked. "This all happened today?"

"I was afraid he'd change his mind. He tends to be quite cautious and meticulous about things, which is one of the reasons I hired him. But if he waits too long, Rose might get away."

Samantha smiled. "Or he might wait until next year to propose..."

William shrugged. "If he's in love with her, why wait?"

Samantha slid closer to her husband and planted a kiss on his cheek. "You care so well for my sisters. It's one of the things I love about you."

"I hope it's all right. I didn't think you'd disapprove."

"I approve of Reuben. And I agree we shouldn't tell Rose, not until we receive the answer from my mother and father. Now, tell me everything Reuben said. What does he think of our Rose?"

"He's not the sort for amorous language, but I could tell he's quite fond of her."

"Did you see his letter before he sent it?"

"No, but I'm sure he's done it justice. He's a far better writer than speaker."

Samantha giggled. "I hope so. Let's be grateful we're so far away so he has to ask by way of letter."

"Shall we go down to supper, then?"

"Yes, but let's train our faces in neutrality," Samantha said with a flare. "Or Rose will know something's amiss."

It was very difficult for Samantha and William to contain their excitement as a whole week passed without any news. Reuben was much better at behaving like normal. You would never guess he had written such a momentous letter to Rose's parents. He continued to dine with them every day at lunch, and sometimes at supper.

In the evenings when he was present, he and Rose would often find themselves alone in the parlor when William and Samantha would sneak off to bed without saying goodnight. Since their schemes were already a known private joke between Rose and Reuben, they'd laugh about it, and continue their talks until it was very late.

On one of these evenings, near a fortnight after Reuben had written his letter, Rose looked around the parlor, hand shielding her eyes as if from the sun. "I can't seem to find William and Samantha. Where do you think they've gone off to?"

Reuben smiled, shadows from the fireplace dancing across his face. "I saw them tiptoeing out about a half hour ago."

Rose sighed dramatically, and sat back. "Mother and Father would reprimand them soundly if they knew how often they left us unchaperoned. That is to say—" Rose stammered. "There is no need—of course..."

"Of course," Reuben soothed. He sunk down in his seat and tilted his head back, becoming easy and relaxed in a way he only seemed to when he and Rose were alone. "You and your sister speak fondly of your parents."

Rose shrugged. "I suppose we do."

"You respect them quite a lot?"

"Yes. They are good parents, as parents go, and they love each other. It's something I've not always seen in couples who've been together for a long time."

Reuben sat forward, curious. "What do you see in them?"

"In their marriage? Well, it's the small things, really. I can tell from their conversation they respect one another. I can tell by the way my father looks at my mother he adores her. My mother still lights up for him. There's a sort of tenderness—a kindness. It's something I've always hoped to find in a marriage—" Rose sucked in her breath, hoping that last statement was not presumptuous, considering she was sitting alone in a parlor with an unmarried man.

When she glanced at Reuben, he was watching her with a strange look in his eyes. It both excited her and made her nervous at the same time. Then he cleared his throat, and Rose's heart flipped inside her chest. "I have something I need to tell you," Reuben said.

Rose's heart began pounding. She was aware Reuben was very fond of her, but he seemed intent on moving slowly and deliberately. She hadn't had time to work out if she'd say yes to a proposal. Could she ask for more time without communicating dissatisfaction with the suitor? Did she like Reuben well enough to marry him? Did he need her father's permission first?

All these thoughts galloped through Rose's head in a matter of seconds.

Reuben spoke softly. "Your parents have invited me to visit Tree Town."

Rose exhaled and inwardly acknowledged she felt both relieved and disappointed. "Oh?" she inquired.

"Yes, and I wanted to ensure you would not mind if I accepted."

"I suppose you may visit whoever you please. When will you go?"

"Whenever you return home with the Temples."

And there Rose's heart began pounding again. "Oh," she whispered.

Reuben tilted his head to gaze at her, his face half shadowed in the firelight. "I wrote to them first," he said. "I said I was fond of you. Their response was an invitation. But I'll not go if you are inclined differently."

Rose stared into the fireplace. As sudden as it was, she was not at all surprised. Her feelings swirled upward and downward inside her. She'd been so amused by the game Samantha and William were playing, she hadn't thought to work out how she felt about Reuben on her own terms.

Her hesitation, she knew, must cause some anxiety for Reuben, who'd clearly determined how he felt about her. But he exuded patience when she looked back at him, waiting for her response with his ever-constant friendship.

So she hated herself for saying, "I believe I might need a day to think on it?"

Reuben nodded once. "Of course. Take all the time you need."

The comfortable silence they enjoyed returned, but Rose's head was buzzing, and she thought she might not sleep at all that night.

As it was, Rose was able to catch a few hours of slumber before dressing and joining Samantha for breakfast. Her sister was just finishing her tea and reading a Herald from Port Town. William had already left for the office.

"I've got something to tell you," said Rose, wringing her hands.

Samantha's head came up with a jolt. Her eyes widened, and she reached for the teapot to pour a cup for Rose.

Rose tried to take a sip, but her hands shook so she placed her cup back in the saucer. Instead, she picked up a piece of toast and took a crunching bite. Through the crumbs she mumbled, "Oogan ants a bisit tee town."

"What was that?" Samantha asked.

Rose swallowed. She took a breath. "Reuben wants to visit Tree Town."

Samantha's face lit up with a grin. "Did he say why?"

"He said he wrote Mother and Father. Told them he was fond of me. And they invited him to visit." Hastily, Rose took another bite of toast.

Samantha's face was still consumed with a smile. She was perturbed Reuben hadn't told William so William could inform her (but she repressed these perturbed feelings). "And...?" she prompted.

"I told him I needed a day to think on it."

"Whatever do you mean?"

Rose spoke in a rush. "There is only one reason Reuben would write our parents to inform them he was fond of me: he means to propose. If Mother and Father invited him to visit, it means they are not against the idea. Considering his friendship with William and his reliable profession, and the fact I am also fond of him, there ought not to be any objections. The only thing is, while I enjoy his company, I hadn't quite worked out if I'd want to *marry* him. And the whole thing seems quite sudden. But if I say yes to the visit, he's likely to take it as encouragement, and I'd hate to say yes to the visit if I'd say no to a proposal."

Rose took another crunching bite of toast.

Samantha let this deluge of verbal thoughts sink in, before saying, "So you would say no if he proposed?"

Rose sighed loudly. "I don't know what I'd say, but I'd hate to encourage him if there is a chance."

Samantha lay the folded Herald on the table and placed her hands on top. "Why would you ever say no?"

"I hadn't thought on it. Like I said, it's very sudden."

"You've been acquainted with Reuben for several months now and have spent almost every day for a month with him here. Surely you can know if you'd want to accept his proposal?"

Rose shrugged and looked around for more toast.

Samantha braced herself. Her intervention was needed. "Tell me all the reasons he would make a good match?"

Rose stared into the distance. "Well, he's kind and a gentleman. He's well-liked by you and William. He's very attentive—I enjoy his company."

"Now tell me the reasons he might not make a good match?"

Rose's eyes widened. "I'm not sure. I suppose he is very quiet, but that is not entirely a flaw. He thinks before he speaks and considers his words carefully."

"Sounds like another reason he'd make a good match."

Rose looked at her sister. "Do *you* think he'd make a good match?"

"No, no, I'll not tell you what to do." Samantha shook her head (though she really wanted to shout "yes!" in her sister's face). "But it does sound like you've already made up your mind, you just don't know it yet."

Rose slumped forward, placing her elbows on the table and her head in her hands. After a moment, she surfaced. "You are right. I do like Reuben. He likes me. There is no reason to not accept a proposal should he be so inclined. I think I'll send him a note right now. When do you think we will be returning home?"

"Why next week, did I not tell you?"

"So soon? Is William's business complete?"

"It will be." But Samantha flushed, knowing she and William had not discussed their return.

But September was soon approaching. If they were going to secure Rose's match and find matches for Elizabeth and Victoria, it was important they return home as soon as possible.

There was little time to lose.

12

Is That Your Definition of Delicate?

Nearly every day for two whole weeks, Daniel exercised Ebony in the field where he'd first encountered Victoria and Elizabeth.

At the end of the two weeks, he was rewarded when he saw them walking along the road, heading home in the afternoon sun.

"Halloo, there!" he called, sliding off his horse and leading the animal to the fence.

Victoria ran over and laid her hand on Ebony's brow.

Elizabeth hung back, eyeing Daniel—and his horse—with suspicion.

"Might I give Ebony a treat?" asked Victoria.

"I suppose."

Victoria retrieved an apple from her pocket, and Ebony swallowed it in two bites. He nudged Victoria affectionately, and Daniel was quite sure the next part of his plan would work.

"Would you like to ride him?" he asked.

Victoria's eyes flooded with stars. Then they dampened immediately. "I don't know how."

"How can that be?" Daniel asked. "All your sisters are proficient."

"I never learned—but I always wanted to."

Daniel witnessed the softening of Elizabeth's rigid form. He thought perhaps she might have a heart after all. He said, "Well today, you shall learn," and offered Victoria his hand.

Victoria bounced over the fence and landed between Ebony and Daniel. She was quite small (for a Hartford) and reminded Daniel of a doll.

If the doll had a tangled mess of unruly hair pinned beneath a straw hat.

Elizabeth came close to the fence. "Stay in this field, please," she said to Daniel.

"You should come, too," he said. "There's plenty of room. I'll lead the horse. It's quite safe."

"I'm not afraid," said Elizabeth. "I do not have riding clothes."

"I don't have riding clothes," Victoria stated. She was staring at the stirrup resting against Ebony's side.

"Suit yourself," said Daniel. He cringed a little, as he'd determined to be as polite to Elizabeth as he could muster.

Ebony fidgeted as Daniel attempted to help Victoria mount. He had to be tied to the fence to keep him steady. Once Victoria was seated on top of the horse, higher above the ground than she had ever been before, she sat board-straight, with a look of dread upon her face. She grasped the saddle and didn't budge.

Daniel smiled up at her. "Relax. Don't be afraid. I won't let Ebony do anything to you."

"Promise you won't let go of him?"

"I promise." He walked forward.

"Slow down!" squealed Victoria. "Remember I've never done this before."

Daniel chuckled. "We're barely walking." He glanced back and saw Victoria had a fistful of Ebony's mane in her hand, squeezing it so tightly her knuckles were white. "Relax, Victoria. You're making him nervous."

"I'm making *him* nervous?" Victoria's eyes were wide.

"You must trust me. Loosen up, all right?" Daniel stopped and gave Victoria a look that demanded her compliance.

Slowly, she exhaled and loosened her grip.

"Just relax," Daniel said coaxingly.

"All right, I will," Victoria muttered. "I'm ready. You can start walking again." Victoria let out her breath and settled in for the ride.

For a moment, they said nothing, meandering around the field encircled by overhanging trees.

"Did you ever play hide and seek in there?" Victoria indicated the woods.

"No."

"What games did you play?"

"None I can remember."

The grass crunched beneath Ebony's hooves as they began another circle around the field. Daniel asked, "Do you want to go a little faster?"

Victoria squeaked a "yes" and Daniel started to jog. Ebony reluctantly complied, and soon Victoria was giggling. When they reached the fence, she called to Elizabeth, "That was so exciting. You should join next time, Bit."

Daniel helped Victoria dismount. When her feet were back on the earth, she smiled up at him. "Thank you, Daniel. May we do it again sometime?"

"Tori," Elizabeth cautioned.

"Whenever you like," Daniel said. "We could ride tomorrow if you want."

"Will you be here tomorrow?"

"Yes."

"Then I will try to come. Now that Rose is engaged, there's nothing to talk about at our house but wedding arrangements."

"What?" Daniel said sharply.

Victoria didn't notice and began climbing over the fence, but Elizabeth rolled her eyes. "It just happened last night, and we weren't supposed to tell anyone yet."

"Daniel will keep it a secret, won't you?" Victoria said.

He exerted great effort in maintaining his composure. "To whom?" he asked, keeping his voice measured.

"Reuben Dudley," Elizabeth said. "He visited William and Samantha this spring."

"They met again at the coast," said Victoria. "He rescued her in a storm and it was very romantic, but she didn't like him at first. Now she's very happy. He's rather handsome, don't you think?"

"Daniel doesn't care if Reuben is handsome," Elizabeth said.

Daniel agreed whole heartedly with Elizabeth, but could only stare straight ahead, quite dumbfounded.

"We'll be off then." Elizabeth looped her arm through Victoria's, pulling her away.

"Goodbye, Daniel. I'll see you tomorrow!"

Daniel barely waved as he placed his foot in the stirrups and swung his leg over Ebony. Heart racing, he took to the woods at a brutal pace.

It was time he paid Samantha another visit.

Rose and Reuben shared an umbrella as they ran through the rain to the greenhouse. Rose fiddled with the latch (it always got stuck on cold, wet days) as water from the roof poured over them.

Once inside, Reuben shook out and closed the umbrella. As he did so, Rose stepped into her world of greenery and flowers, inhaling the moisture of combined scents.

She wondered if her home with Reuben at the coast would have room for a garden. They hadn't discussed what part of Port Town they intended to live in, but they'd likely find a small house in place of Reuben's bachelor apartment. She was already planning her trousseau, and the home in her head was very cozy and comforting.

And Reuben was in it, which was both strange and exciting.

She was *engaged*.

And just a few months earlier, she hadn't even known Reuben existed.

"You grew all this?" Reuben's voice brought Rose back to the present.

She turned around to face him. He hadn't fully escaped the downpour, and his coat was wet on the shoulders and tail. His dark hair curled around his face—a result of the damp air.

"Yes, mostly me," Rose said. "My mother assists with the herbs, but the shrubs. The flowers. These are mine."

Rose bent to inhale the scent of the flower that was her namesake. She was most proud of her large red roses and would likely have an abundance of them at her wedding.

Reuben had moved closer, observing her as she observed her foliage.

Rose straightened. "I want to have a garden," she said, without looking at her intended.

Reuben said, "All right." He appeared to know she was talking about their future home.

"And a room for painting." She turned toward him, suddenly feeling her demands were very important. "I don't intend to give up painting. It's always been more than a pastime to me, and I intend for it to remain that way."

Reuben tilted his head to the side, not answering right away. The intensity of his gaze caused Rose to turn back to her roses.

Then Reuben was beside her, standing very close. Taking her hand, he drew her around to face him. Rose forced herself to look in his eyes, though she wanted very much to cower away.

She'd already said yes to his lovely proposal of

marriage, and she knew her whole family approved.

But while she stood in the most sacred space of her unmarried life, the reality of the change overwhelmed her.

Reuben placed a hand on Rose's cheek, eyes focused on hers, as if he were trying to read her thoughts. It felt like instinct, when Rose covered his hand with her own, and took one step closer so her body was just barely pressed up against his. She sensed he wanted to kiss her, but was holding back for a question.

"Are you happy, Rose?" he finally asked.

"Yes," she answered without thinking.

"No, I mean..." He hesitated, searching for words. "Are you happy with *me*?"

Rose ducked her chin. "Of course," she sighed.

"Then," Reuben's gaze grew more intense. "What is it you're afraid of?"

Rose sagged slightly. Until he'd asked the question, she hadn't even known she was afraid. But the moment he had, she knew with certainty the reason, and it came out in a rush. "I'm afraid of losing myself. All I've ever known and loved is here. It's all I ever wanted. I *do* love you. I just don't know how to do this—how to stay me when I'm with you. I don't know what it looks like or what it's supposed to feel like. Does this make any sense at all?"

Reuben wrapped his arms around her and Rose relaxed into his embrace, feeling like he understood her, even if she didn't fully understand herself.

"I don't think what you're saying is uncommon for couples," Reuben said gently. "But I have no doubt we'll figure it out. Together. I love you. And I can't imagine wanting you to change who you are, just because we're getting married." Something very vulnerable flashed behind Reuben's eyes, and his breath came out shakily. "That is—if you still want to get married."

Rose felt Reuben's hold on her body loosen, but instead of relinquishing her, he stayed close. Rose reached up and gripped the lapels on his coat. "Oh, you're not getting rid of me that easily." She smiled.

Reuben's answering smile caused the corners of his eyes to crinkle in the way Rose had come to adore. She suddenly couldn't stand any space between them, and she tugged on his coat until his mouth was on hers.

For several days following, she blushed every time she recalled how passionately they'd kissed inside the greenhouse.

Daniel headed to town with the alacrity of a man on a mission. He planned to surprise Samantha with a visit, and though he wasn't supposed to know about Rose's engagement, he would make it very clear he was already apprised of the situation.

His plans were stunted when, the moment he entered town, he saw Samantha, with a basket draped over her arm, heading to the grocers.

William must be very poor indeed if Samantha had no servant to attend the market on her behalf.

Just as she was about to enter, Daniel came up

short just behind her. Losing all restraint, he said, "I hear congratulations are in order for our dear sister Rose."

Samantha froze. She turned around. "How—how did you hear about that?"

Daniel's pride swelled. "I have my ways."

Samantha collected herself. "Well, it is not public knowledge yet, so I'll thank you to keep it to yourself."

"Of course, of course," Daniel said. "But you must tell me your secret. How did you manage to trick another man into marrying one of your sisters?"

Samantha laughed (but it was forced). "Getting nervous?" She nodded toward the grocers' door, and Daniel leaned around to open it for her.

"Not at all," he answered, as they both entered the store. "While you certainly had a stroke of luck with Allison—and now with Rose—you're in over your head with Elizabeth and Victoria. Victoria is barely a woman, and Elizabeth—well—let's say, her disposition—I'll be delicate—it's a bit off-putting."

"Is that your definition of delicate?"

"Come, come Samantha. Admit it. You have no prospects for either of them, and it's September. No one can work a miracle—least of all you—and your youngest sisters are the most difficult of all."

"Is that all you came to say? That you think we shall lose by-and-by?"

"I don't *think* you will lose, I know you will."

"Then I see no point in continuing this conversation."

"I see no point in continuing the challenge. I'll be a gentleman and accept your defeat whenever you and the dashing Mr. Temple are ready."

"Sounds to me as if you're getting nervous."

"Let me see, what would be a good title for the article you will write about me..."

"Yes, it sounds very much as if you're trying to save face."

"I don't need to save face. I'm not a member of the family who's thrown off convention and thereby warded off eligible bachelors for years. If you ask me, I've done you a favor by giving you incentive to *need* husbands for your sisters. Now they won't be quite the blight on society they've been in the past."

Samantha rounded on Daniel, basket swinging dangerously close to his chest. "That is quite enough. I do not wish to speak with you anymore today."

The swelling of Daniel's bravado sunk with force. In the face of Samantha's genuine disgust, he paled, jaw working to form words. He became aware he was standing inside the grocers (a place he hadn't entered since he was a child) and looked around for something to do, before stating, "I believe I have some unattended business. I'll be going then." He swiveled about and left the shop in a rush, face flushing hot and stomach brimming with an uncomfortable knot.

13

Don't Make it Too Large

Samantha stood trembling where Daniel had left her, basket handle twisting in her grip. Mr. Cole startled her when he asked, "Everything all right, Samantha?"

Samantha tried to smile, but the look on Mr. Cole's face told he had witnessed what transpired between her and Daniel, and this caused her to feel ashamed of how sharply she'd spoken. "You know, I quite forgot what I came in here for."

Mr. Cole's concern deepened. "May I help?"

"No, no," Samantha laughed nervously. "I'll return when I remember. Do tell your mother hello?"

Mr. Cole watched her leave. While he'd not heard what either Samantha or Daniel had said, whatever it was had deeply upset Samantha. He'd half a mind to go after Daniel and give him a stern reprimand, but he and Daniel had never been on friendly terms. Their only interaction was at town functions. Considering Mr. Cole was of the working class while Daniel was from a very old aristocratic line, there had never been much occasion for anything more than an indifferent acquaintance.

Still, Edward Cole remained transfixed, debating whether he should come to Samantha's aid, when a bit of movement caught his eye, and Allison Hartford slid into the aisle.

He'd forgotten she'd entered the grocers nearly two hours earlier.

She glanced at Mr. Cole, sighed heavily, then proceeded out the door.

Instead of turning left to follow Samantha, however, she turned right and headed toward her home at a rapid pace.

Mr. Cole returned to dusting the shelves.

Allison detested wedding planning. All was well and good when she and Ethan were hoping for a small ceremony once their house was finally built, but the moment Rose became engaged, everything changed. Rose adored fashion and flowers and beautiful things. She was also the most romantic of all the sisters, and her desire for a grand event was palpable. Their mother fed her frenzy and there was nothing but wedding talk floating about any room Allison entered.

It was also harvest time—the busiest season on the estate—and Allison barely had an uninterrupted moment.

Mr. Cole had always been a friend and always kept a small collection of books at his store. There was a small nook between two shelves where Allison could hide from the world, and she'd often make her escape when time allowed.

Considering no one in town yet knew of Rose's engagement, Allison was certain she wouldn't be accosted by any of the town busybodies. She'd already disappointed Alma Burros greatly when she'd given no details of her marriage plans when asked. She'd also gotten riled when Mrs. Vaughn and Mrs. Sommers indicated Ethan was beneath her in class, and shouldn't she wait until someone of greater wealth and status should come along?

It had taken every ounce of self-control for Allison to keep her cool.

All that to say, on one of these occasions of escape, Allison happened to be inside *Cole & Family Household Goods* when Daniel and Samantha entered. Her perch had been just two aisles over, and she'd heard their entire conversation.

The moment the coast was clear, she set out for home. Determined to tell the tale to the people it most concerned.

It took Allison nearly half an hour to find Rose, and she cursed herself for not thinking to look in the hothouse first. Rose was creating floral demonstrations and inquired of her breathless sister if she thought there were too many roses in the arrangement.

Allison leaned forward and gripped a stitch in her side. "We need to find Ethan, and I need to speak to both of you at once."

Rose's eyes widened. "What has happened?"

"Never mind, I'll tell you once we've found Ethan."

Allison took Rose's arm and hauled her toward the field where Ethan worked nearly every evening on the house he and Allison would live in once they were married.

He spotted them coming and jumped down from the pile of wood near the foundation.

"Everything all right?" he asked casually.

Both Allison and Rose took a moment to catch their breaths, then Allison blurted out. "Samantha and William have been conspiring with Daniel Copeland to see all the sisters married this year."

Rose and Ethan looked at one another. "What do you mean, conspiring?" Rose asked.

Allison stood up straight. "I overheard them in the grocers. Apparently, William and Samantha made some sort of deal with Daniel and they're trying to see us all matched. They were arguing about Victoria and Elizabeth. Daniel said they'd be the most difficult and that William and Samantha got lucky with my match and Rose's."

Rose paled.

Ethan crossed his arms, looking stern.

"Why—why would they do that?" Rose stammered.

"Who knows? But with *Daniel Copeland*. The boy is an irritation. So cynical and so critical of us. Samantha's always been friendly with him, but I could never see why. Now she's gone and made a deal with him—involving us. I just can't believe it."

Rose chewed her bottom lip. "I can't believe it either. Ought we to inquire of Samantha the details of this arrangement? Perhaps there's something we do not understand?"

"Oh, the intent was quite clear."

"But we don't know why," Rose said loyally. "Perhaps there is a reason."

"But tampering with our futures? It's ghastly."

"Yes, which is why we need to find out what's going on before we judge William and Samantha too harshly. And I'm afraid I won't be able to sleep tonight if I do not know. Let's go there immediately."

Allison turned to Ethan, who'd said nothing so far. "And you?" she asked. "What do you think of this?"

Ethan glanced at his feet. "I don't see how they had anything to do with our engagement."

"That is why Daniel said they got lucky."

Rose paled further. "Reuben..." she whispered.

"They brought him here. Even before Ethan returned."

"They wanted him to fall in love with one of us."

"Looks like they got their wish."

Rose looked like she was about to faint, and Ethan took her arm to steady her.

Allison sobered. "Oh Rose, you don't think they pushed you into your engagement, do you? You seem so happy."

"Am I?" Rose asked. "Or was it all by design?"

"I say," said Ethan. "Let's not be hasty. Let us hear Samantha and William's defense."

"Right," Allison declared. "Off to town we go. Can you walk Rose?"

"I'll be fine." She straightened. "Are you coming, Ethan?"

"Afraid not." He indicated the pile of wood behind him. "Your father said I can't marry Allison until this house is built. Pact with Daniel Copeland or not, I'm not waiting a minute longer than I have to."

Allison stepped toward him and planted a kiss on his stubbled cheek. "Don't make it too large." She took Rose's hand, and the two sisters set off for town.

The sun was setting behind them when they arrived at Tree Town. The little village was quieting down for the night, and Rose and Allison refrained from speaking until they were on Samantha and William's doorstep.

"They'll likely be alarmed when they see us," said Rose.

"Let them be alarmed, we're the ones with a bone to pick."

"Allison, do you have to always be so crass?"

"Now is not the time for a lesson in manners."

The door opened and instead of William and Samantha, a woman they did not recognize stood before them. "Yes?" the woman said kindly.

"Samantha Temple?" Allison asked, looking around to ensure she had the right house.

"Oh, you must be the sisters!" The woman smiled, one of those smiles that covered her face in affectionate wrinkles. "I've been instructed to never bar entrance to a sister. Come in, come in."

Allison and Rose crossed the threshold.

"I'm Mrs. Bishop, the housekeeper," the woman explained.

"Samantha didn't tell us she was procuring a housekeeper," said Rose.

"I just arrived." The woman chuckled. "Come in here. Mr. and Mrs. Temple are in the parlor."

As they followed Mrs. Bishop, Allison whispered, "Mr. and Mrs. Temple?" and Rose snorted a laugh.

When they entered the parlor, they saw Samantha and William seated on the sofa.

Samantha wore a downtrodden look upon her face. William was turned toward her, holding her hand, but withdrew and stood to greet the sisters. Samantha smiled, but it was a sad smile.

As they took their seats, Rose whispered to Allison, "Maybe this isn't a good time." Allison whispered back, "It's never a good time for these sorts of things." She began: "Samantha, I think that you should know, I overheard your conversation with Daniel Copeland in the grocers earlier today."

Samantha blinked several times. "Overheard it? How?"

"I was reading. It all happened quite fast."

Samantha's shoulders drooped. "How much did you hear?"

"Everything you said from the moment you entered. I know you've made some sort of deal with Daniel to see us married—or something—anyway, we wanted to tell you the jig is up and we're here to find out what you have to say for yourselves."

Samantha and William sat side by side, very still, and both stared at the floor, like two school children who'd just been caught pulling a prank during class.

Finally, Samantha spoke, "It was all in good fun. Until it wasn't anymore."

William placed a comforting hand on Samantha's shoulder.

"Fun?" Rose said. "It was fun to tamper with our hearts and futures?"

Samantha was stricken. "Nothing like that. We both determined we couldn't make any of you fall in love, we merely sought to create opportunities."

"But you encouraged me to say yes if Reuben proposed."

Samantha's eyes suddenly filled with tears. "Rose, dear, Rose, I never meant to put pressure on you. Do you feel you've said yes too hastily?"

Rose inhaled slowly.

Bracing himself, William took Samantha's hand. "I'll confess my own part in that. I encouraged Reuben to write to your mother and father."

Rose glanced up sharply. "So not even that was his idea?"

William grimaced. "I felt he'd get there eventually. I merely sought to help him along."

Rose squared off with her sister and brother-in-law. "Tell me plainly, would you have encouraged this so strongly if there hadn't been a bet with Daniel?"

Samantha and William looked at one another. Samantha said, "Not with quite so much enthusiasm, no."

After a very heavy silence, William said, "Rose, we are sincerely sorry if we caused you pain. We care far more about your happiness than about winning the wager with Daniel. Please accept our apology, and if you wish to call off your engagement, you have our support."

Rose stared at the hands clasped in her lap. Finally, she heaved a heavy sigh. "The truth is, I do love Reuben. There were moments I felt like things were moving awfully fast and I wasn't sure I knew my own heart. But when I think of *not* marrying Reuben—I—I just cannot fathom it. However, he will have to be told about this, and he may not feel the same way."

"I bet my life, he won't change his mind," William said, with a bit more alacrity. "But I'll write to him and tell him the role we played."

Rose smiled. "Your designs were not completely hidden from us. We were aware you were trying to throw us together, and it became a bit of a joke—until Reuben told me he'd written to Mother and Father. I hadn't thought seriously about marrying him, but without your efforts, I wonder now if I ever would have. While I don't like feeling like a pawn, I can't deny the result was still favorable."

Samantha scooted to the edge of her seat and said urgently. "We never would have encouraged if we hadn't thought you both already fond of one another."

"I believe you," said Rose. "And I forgive you both."

At that precise moment, Mrs. Bishop entered the room with a tray. "My scones were for the morning," she said jovially. "But I think you'll be needing them tonight." As she placed the tray on the table, she glanced up and winked at Rose and Allison before departing.

Allison rested her forearms on her knees. "Now, tell us about Daniel Copeland—why on earth did you make this arrangement in the first place?"

Samantha reached for the pot of tea. "It happened rather quickly. He came to visit after we returned from the honeymoon trip and was his usual cynical self, declaring the only reason I found a husband was because I was lucky and that no other man would ever be so foolish as to marry any of my sisters. Somehow, we made a wager, stating if all my sisters were engaged by the end of the year, then he would make speeches at each of your weddings singing your praises. If we lose, we're to write an article in The Post, doing the same for him."

Allison and Rose's eyes were wide as Samantha handed them cups of tea. "It started out as good fun, but after today, I don't have the heart to continue. Let Daniel crow his victory. I'm quite done with matchmaking."

Allison stiffened. "Sounds to me Daniel deserved everything you said. He insulted Victoria and Elizabeth—nay, he insulted our whole family!"

"That's what I've been telling Samantha all evening," said William. "His behavior was abominable."

"But that's just it." Samantha leaned back against the sofa. "I've always felt sorry for Daniel. Though he can be very rude, I've never thought it came from a place of unkindness—just—I believe he's lonely and lacks an ambition to occupy his time. He had a fine education, but I don't believe he was really brought up well. I always thought, with a little encouragement, he might turn out all right. But I think this wager has made him worse, and I think it's driven away any influence I might have had over him."

Rose sipped her tea delicately before saying, "It is not your fault Daniel is the way he is."

"No, but it's my fault for rising to his jibes."

Allison rested her saucer on her knees. "I think

there's only one thing left to do. See the bet through to the end."

"Weren't you offended when you found out what we were up to?" Samantha asked.

"Of course, until I heard why you did it. It might be impossible, but we have to at least try. It'll do the boy good to experience defeat of this magnitude. Now, who did you have in mind for Tori and Bit?"

"That's just it. Daniel was partly right. We have absolutely no ideas for either of them."

"Got anymore friends hidden away, William?"

William chuckled. "None with the heart and character of Reuben." He smiled at Rose.

"Then we need to start scheming. I'll ask Ethan if he has any ideas."

"And I'll write to Reuben for his advice," said Rose.

"Wait a minute," said Samantha. "I don't want us to get carried away. I'd already determined to surrender, even before you two arrived. It's become too serious."

"Don't you see," said Allison. "If you lose, it'll only make Daniel worse."

"But *marriage*. It's altogether too important to be a game."

"Besides," said Rose. "When did we turn into the family who can only think of marriage and husbands?"

"You're one to talk," said Allison. "You haven't stopped thinking of marriage and weddings since Reuben proposed."

"I'm entitled to it, aren't I?"

"Of course. And don't you want the same happiness for your sisters?"

Rose tapped her lips with a finger. "You're right.

The least we can do is *try* to find matches. Like you both said earlier, we can't make anyone fall in love. We just need to create opportunities."

"But isn't this against the rules?" Samantha looked at her husband for support, but William was grinning mischievously, and she knew he'd been snagged into the game again. "We forfeit if we tell anyone."

"You didn't tell us," said Allison. "In fact, I believe Daniel was the one who revealed the information when he accosted you."

Samantha conceded this was true.

Allison rose up a little in her seat. "I think I might enjoy this. With the four of us on the trail, Daniel doesn't stand a chance." She raised her teacup as a toast. "To the utter defeat and humiliation of Daniel Copeland."

Rose and William joined her, and they all glanced at Samantha.

"Come on, Sam," said Rose. "We need you."

With great reluctance, Samantha peeled herself away from the sofa and lifted her cup. "To my sisters, who never cease to make me very proud."

"To us!" Rose cheered.

Their glasses clinked together, confirming the addition of two more players to the game.

14

We're Merely Creating Opportunities

Outside the brick edifice that served as the town hall and town chapel, Daniel Copeland watched a little scene transpire. Samantha and William exited the church. They were followed by Mr. and Mrs. Hartford. Then came Mr. Cole, the grocer. They greeted the pastor with handshakes and smiles. Then Mr. Cole tipped his hat and began to walk away. Mr. Hartford called after him and invited him to join Sunday luncheon. Mr. Cole accepted, and the party began to walk in the direction of the Hartford estate.

Those whom Daniel observed next were connected with the previous party. Rose and Allison exited the church and spoke with the pastor. They laughed at something the pastor said, then they continued on, whispering as they cast glances after their parents, sister, brother-in-law, and the strongly built form of Mr. Cole.

Victoria and Elizabeth were next, and caught up with their older sisters. The four young women stopped at the edge of the lane and waited for Ethan, who supported his aunt as she spoke with the pastor. Then the sisters, Aunt Letty, and Ethan formed a happy band as they headed for home.

Daniel pulled his cap further down upon his head and brooded. Something else was going to happen. He was sure it concerned Mr. Cole or the man wouldn't have been invited over to the Hartford home. At least this is what Daniel told himself. Inwardly, he acknowledged the Hartfords constantly invited guests to their home.

There could be nothing to it. But still, Daniel had a feeling.

He sauntered off to amuse himself in what way he could on that Sunday afternoon, though his mood was growing considerably more sour with every passing moment.

Daniel was not wrong about Mr. Cole and events developing around him. During the service, Allison had suddenly noticed Mr. Cole, sitting not far off in his family pew (where he nearly always sat alone, as his mother continued to decline in health). Bursting with sudden inspiration, Allison leaned over and whispered to her father and mother, "Invite Mr. Cole to luncheon."

Mr. and Mrs. Hartford nodded acceptance. They hadn't conversed with Mr. Cole in months and always enjoyed the gentleman's company.

Allison sat back with a satisfied smile.

Rose whispered, "What are you up to?" to her sister.

"Just an idea. One I don't know I would have ever considered, had we not a challenge to win."

"Allison..." Rose cautioned. But Allison silenced her with a wave of the hand.

As they departed Sunday service and headed for home, Allison decided to test the waters with Elizabeth. "I'm delighted Mr. Cole is coming to lunch. He's one of my favorite people in the whole world. Do not you think so, Elizabeth?"

Rose gave Allison a warning poke in the side.

"I supposed." Elizabeth sighed.

"You've always been fond of Mr. Cole—and his mother." Allison continued to probe.

"I've done my Christian duty and visited her every month. Even when my sisters were too busy."

"Then," said Rose. "You don't actually *like* Mrs. Cole?"

"Like is unimportant when it is one's duty."

With the completion of this second Sunday sermon, the sisters walked on in silence, trailed by Ethan and Aunt Letty, who were having a much more pleasant conversation about fireflies.

The minds of Allison and Rose were kept busy during the afternoon. Elizabeth's comment about Mr. Cole and his mother had caught them both unawares, as they had no reason to believe Elizabeth held anything but deep respect for them both. Indeed, they witnessed her paying particular attention to everything he said (but both concluded they might have imagined it).

They watched Mr. Cole for signs of special affection for Elizabeth, but nothing other than brotherly kindness could be discerned. He was attentive to all the sisters equally. How he'd managed it throughout the years was marvelous. Allison and Rose acknowledged later they had never thought their friendship with a town grocer strange. When it came to Mr. Cole, there was no hypocrisy, no pretense, no flaw in any of his mannerisms.

After he'd been thoroughly scrutinized, Allison and Rose wondered if any woman in the world was worthy of Mr. Cole.

Furthermore, the job of matchmaking was proving more difficult than they had imagined. Their creative scheming ended in absurdities. They could not think of an auspicious way to bring Elizabeth and Mr. Cole into an acquaintance beyond friendship.

The next day, Rose dispatched a note to Reuben, and Allison sought out Ethan for help. When first Ethan heard of it, he laughed outright, but quickly sobered when he realized his intended was serious. "Edward Cole is too old," he said.

"He's twenty-eight. Eight years in age is not too much."

"All right, he *seems* too old. Besides, Elizabeth is so beautiful. I'd think she'd want someone more dashing, don't you?"

"Mr. Cole is handsome. It just comes on gradually as you get to know him."

"I've known him all my life, and I've never heard him referred to as handsome."

"He's had a difficult time of it. He had to grow up much faster than most of us, what with the death of his father and the illness of his mother. I think he might like a wife. I consider it our Christian duty to provide one for him."

Ethan laughed again. "By all means, offer him Elizabeth. I'm sure he won't say no. But don't you think Elizabeth a bit too fashionable for a grocer's wife?"

"It's a respectable trade."

"It's working class."

"You're working class, you know?"

Ethan grinned. "Yes, and I already have a wife."

"Not yet," said Allison. "I could still change my mind."

"If it's in the cards, do so quickly, building that house is a great burden."

Allison stepped closer to him. "Are you complaining?"

"Never. I love building our house. Love it with all my soul. Perhaps I'll marry it instead."

Allison leaned forward to kiss him, but just before their lips touched, she cried, "Samantha! I have to ask Samantha what she thinks of Mr. Cole and Elizabeth." She bolted away, leaving Ethan staring after her.

"Edward Cole is too old," Samantha said. She was dictating instructions to Mrs. Bishop about household duties while she and William were away at the coast. "These clothes need to be mended," she said, placing a pile in Mrs. Bishop's arms. She walked on, followed by the housekeeper and Rose and Allison, who'd arrived with lights in their eyes just as she was beginning.

"He's only twenty-eight. Just eight years older than Elizabeth," said Allison.

"Really? Is that all?" Samantha moved down her list without glancing up.

"Don't you find it strange we've never thought of Mr. Cole as a suitor before?" Rose said.

"I suppose we never had a reason to," Samantha pointed out.

"If Elizabeth were to marry someone closer to her age, he likely wouldn't be established in a profession yet. She'll have to marry someone older, anyways."

"Why Elizabeth and not Victoria?" Samantha stepped into the kitchen and began going through the stores, pointing to items that needed replacing. Mrs. Bishop made a jot on her pad of paper.

"Victoria *is* much too young for Mr. Cole," said Rose. "Elizabeth has always been thought mature for her age. Besides, she already has a connection to Mr. Cole through his mother."

"I cannot see Victoria caring for Mr. Cole and his mother the same way Elizabeth would," Allison added.

"Why would you wish to see Elizabeth burdened with the care of Mrs. Cole?" said Samantha.

"Why should Mr. Cole not marry because of his unfortunate situation?" Allison responded.

"Indeed," said Rose. "It might be the reason he has never married. It's just like him to not wish to place such a burden on a wife. He's a kind, generous soul. He deserves a good wife."

"And why should that wife be Elizabeth?" Samantha sank into a chair at the kitchen table and Mrs. Bishop began preparing tea. "She has so many admirers at the coast. She could have a much more dashing fellow, I'm sure."

"Those snobs?" Allison scoffed. "Never."

"We have to at least try," said Rose, as she and Allison sat across from Samantha. "They'll likely never look at one another in that way unless someone helps them along."

Samantha waited for Rose to express some word of caution or hesitation, but she was just as enraptured with the idea as Allison. All ill-will for Samantha and William's manipulation in her relationship with Reuben was forgotten.

Indeed, Rose guessed what Samantha was thinking and said, "We're merely creating opportunities."

Samantha sighed and placed her list on the table. "But they've had a lifetime of opportunities. Why now?"

Allison threw up her hands. "Because we have a bet to win. Isn't that obvious?"

Mrs. Bishop placed teacups in front of the women and the pot in front of Samantha, then she retreated with the pile of clothes. Samantha started to reach for the pot, but Rose snatched it up. "You seem very tired Samantha, are you ill?"

"No," she responded. "But all the trips back and forth to the coast are beginning to take their toll."

"Have you thought of moving to the coast?" Allison asked.

Samantha sipped her tea. "We've not made any arrangements, but yes, it's something I fear we will have to consider."

The sisters became sober.

"I would like that," said Rose. "As happy as I am with the prospect of marrying Reuben, I am deeply sad about living so far from family. If you were in town also, my heart would just melt."

"Well, we'll not make any final plans until the spring," Samantha said. "But it would do my heart good to know I'll not be leaving all my family behind."

"Harvest!" Allison declared, startling both Rose and Samantha so they spilled their tea. "The final day of Harvest is the perfect time to throw Elizabeth and Mr. Cole together."

The last day of Harvest, everyone in Tree Town turned out at the Hartford estate to help prepare the final stores. At the end of the day, large fires burned on the hillside and there would be laughing and dancing until dawn.

It was one of the most looked-forward to days of the year for the entire community.

Samantha smiled. "It would be a lovely time, but Edward's attendance has always been unpredictable, because of his mother."

"We will just have to ensure he comes this year," said Rose.

"Yes, perhaps we can find someone willing to sit with Mrs. Cole in the event she has a bad spell."

Mrs. Bishop poked her head in the kitchen. "A parcel just arrived for you ma'am, I placed it in the parlor."

The sisters stared at Mrs. Bishop and had the same idea. "Mrs. Bishop, we are in need of a favor," said Allison.

Rose took hold of Mrs. Bishop's hand and drew her close to the table.

15

You Must Be So Delighted

Victoria was waiting in the field when Daniel arrived with Ebony. "No Elizabeth today?" he asked.

Victoria shrugged. "She didn't think I should come without a chaperone."

Daniel dismounted Ebony near the fence. "And you disagree?"

"I'm here, aren't I?"

Daniel helped Victoria into Ebony's saddle. "I brought a lead today, so you can take the reins and I'll be here just in case."

"Really?" Victoria was delighted. He showed her how to hold the straps in her hands and off they went. "Might we see more of your home?" she asked.

"Give her the reins and she asks for the world," Daniel said. He smiled at her and she smiled back. "Take him wherever you want."

Victoria guided the horse toward one of the wooded trails. Surrounded by the density of the trees, everything became quiet. The only sound was the crunch of hooves on the path. Several minutes into the ride, Daniel asked, "How come you never learned to ride?"

"I suppose everyone just got busy. But really, I never said I wanted to learn."

"Why?"

"I just figured everyone had better things to do."

Daniel tucked this detail away, delighted to have uncovered a flaw in Hartford bliss.

"Your land is truly magnificent," Victoria said.

Daniel cleared his throat. Though he'd always been aware of their acres and acres of land, "magnificent" wasn't a descriptor he had ever used.

"What do you do with all of it?" she asked.

Daniel coughed. "Well, I'd thought about lending it out to people who'd want to farm it."

"That's a wonderful idea!"

Daniel was slightly startled by such a display of affirmation.

"When will you begin?" she asked.

"Oh, it was just an idea, one I'm afraid my mother does not approve of."

"For what reason?" she asked.

"For her own reasons I cannot fathom."

"I am very sorry. I do think you'd like being a landlord."

Daniel didn't respond, but the idea of liking responsibility had never quite occurred to him.

They returned to the field. As Daniel helped Victoria dismount, she asked, "Will you be coming to Harvest?"

"Is that this week?"

"Yes. You always come."

"Do I? Then yes, I suppose I'll be there."

"Wonderful!" Victoria exclaimed. "I'll be so happy to have you there. With all my sisters preoccupied with their engagements—it'll be nice to have a friend."

"Wait a minute," Daniel became stern. "*All* your sisters?"

Victoria laughed. "Not Elizabeth. But that would be strange wouldn't it? You'd think there was some sort of magic in the air, all these engagements happening so quickly."

"Yes. Magic," Daniel grunted.

Victoria proceeded to climb the fence. She stumbled on the other side and her hat slipped down. She chuckled and pushed it back.

"Tell Elizabeth to come next time," Daniel drawled. "I missed her charming countenance."

"With Harvest just a few days away, I doubt she'll come. We're all exceedingly busy."

"Oh, well, do you want to pick this up later then?" Immediately after he said it, he wanted to take it back. Keeping Victoria and Elizabeth occupied was his only sure way of winning the bet—though he wasn't so sure it was still on, after his last encounter with Samantha.

"Only if you're becoming bored with me," said Victoria. "It's nice to have a reason to escape all the bustle."

"Your family does not mind?"

"My family doesn't notice."

After Victoria disappeared down the road, Daniel

took Ebony into the woods. He gave the horse some good exercise, as he thought about the upcoming Harvest Day.

Perhaps he'd pay more attention this year. Perhaps next year, he might have a harvest of his own, on his own land.

Quickly, he cleared his mind of the hope. His mother's refusal to use the land for anything other than status and a display of wealth was an obstacle he would not easily surmount.

He returned Ebony to the stables. As he headed back into the house, his stomach dropped with a realization.

Samantha would be at Harvest Day. He hadn't seen her since their scuffle. Likely William knew all about it, too. Though Daniel was inclined to play it off as if it had never happened, he knew, with unusual acuity, that the row had been his fault.

He desperately wanted to wish it away as part of the game, but unfortunately he hadn't been able to do that. His stomach formed into an uncomfortable knot any time he thought on it. He did not like the uncomfortable knot, so he chose to ignore it with distraction.

But seeing Samantha at her family's home would most likely tighten the knot to beyond unbearable.

Elizabeth stomped down the road to Tree Town, a basket swinging angrily by her side. This trip to the grocers was unnecessary, considering how much they all had to do before Harvest Day, and she was sure Allison had something to do with it.

Mrs. Hartford had announced she needed some last minute things from town and was about to hand a list to their maid, Rebecca, when Allison interjected. Elizabeth was preoccupied with counting jars in the storeroom and did not hear the conversation, but within a few seconds, she was being shoved out the door in the direction of town.

"Why can't one of the servants go? What do we have them for if not for small errands?"

"Don't be a snob, Bit," said Allison. "We always go to the grocers. Honestly, what would Mr. Cole think if we sent Rebecca for goods instead of coming ourselves?"

"I don't care what Mr. Cole thinks," Elizabeth said (though this was entirely untrue).

"Go on," Allison said, shooing Elizabeth away. "Tell Edward we'll see him on Saturday."

Elizabeth rolled her eyes and began her march into town.

Of course they would see him on Saturday, she thought to herself. Ever since Edward Cole had joined them for luncheon two weeks earlier, Rose and Allison seemed to bring him up in every conversation. It was like they didn't remember they were both engaged and supposed to be planning weddings, though the wedding planning had gone on temporary hold as Harvest Day drew closer.

The grocers came into view and Elizabeth picked up her pace. The sooner she could get all her mother's requirements, the sooner she could return home.

The door to the grocers swung open.

Elizabeth froze, but it was too late to escape. She couldn't pretend she hadn't seen the woman, as they'd nearly collided.

"Elizabeth Hartford!" Alma Burros said. "What's brought you into town? Shopping for the upcoming weddings? I'm sure your house is full of such joy and celebration, considering how we all thought none of you young ladies would ever marry. But now look! Three engagements in one year. I don't quite understand why Rose is waiting so long to get married. I understand Ethan and Allison must wait until he has an established profession, but I don't see him doing much on that score, do you? Oh never mind, I'm just so happy for you all. You must be delighted to know your older sisters are getting married, as it paves the way for you, my dear. Honestly, you were the only sister I ever held out hope for. You're so lovely, I can't imagine you'll be single for long. Now all the men will just fall in line. You must be so delighted!" Alma Burros chortled. Though her hands were full of parcels, she turned around to follow Elizabeth into the store.

Trying to signal the end of the conversation, Elizabeth said, "Thank you for your kind wishes toward my family. I do hope we'll see you Saturday." She took several long strides inside the grocers, but somehow Alma's short legs kept pace, and she remained right on Elizabeth's heels.

"How strange your family is for sending you to the grocers. I've always wondered why you all come on your own. Surely your family has servants for such things? But then again, your family always was so strange—what with Allison running the estate and you all being so educated. I've always thought the more knowledge a woman has the more difficult it would be for her to find a husband. If a man has to work too hard to remain more intelligent than his wife, it makes it very difficult for him to remain the head of his home. Better for a woman to have just enough knowledge to keep her home and raise her children to be proper young people—and leave the rest to the man, don't you think so? I was so concerned for your sister Allison. Not that her marriage is anything noteworthy. But Rose! Dear Rose. She truly is a rare flower. I know nothing about her young man, but he is exceedingly handsome. You're going to have quite a time of it, making a match to compete with your sister's, but I have high hopes for you, yes I really do." Alma Burros beamed, and Elizabeth had to slide past her to get to the next aisle.

With sinking stomach, Elizabeth realized one of the items on the list would require Mr. Cole to enter the storeroom. She could not for the life of her understand why her mother needed just that much cheesecloth, and it wasn't an item Mr. Cole kept on the main shelves. She glanced around for him, as Alma continued to prattle.

Mr. Cole appeared on the landing near his living quarters. He looked flushed, and Elizabeth wondered if this meant his mother wasn't having a good day. As he descended the stairs, Elizabeth felt awful for having to ask him for the item, but her look of apology as she made her request was completely missed by Mr. Cole, who barely looked at her before heading back into the storeroom.

Elizabeth saw her escape from Alma Burros. "I'm to visit Mr. Cole's mother, Mrs. Burros. Would you like to join me?"

"Oh no, oh no, I've got so much to do. I'll see you Saturday?" She shuffled away so quickly Elizabeth was spared having to say goodbye.

Though it wasn't the first week of the month, she felt sure Mr. Cole would appreciate her looking in on his mother. The poor man was burdened with the store and the care of his mother. He hardly had a moment's peace. No one knew this better than she, for she'd been coming regularly to visit the invalid Mrs. Cole for years.

She was quite possibly the only person in town who knew Mrs. Cole's health had been on a slow decline all year.

Elizabeth usually knocked, but she thought Mrs. Cole might be sleeping, so she took hold of the knob and slowly turned it. Just as the door was ajar enough to see Mrs. Cole drooped in her usual chair, the door slammed in her face. She whirled around as Mr. Cole finished securing it, shoving the cheesecloth into her arms. "Is there anything else I can help you with?" His tone was harsher than she'd ever heard it, and Elizabeth twisted past him to create space between him and the door.

"I've just a few more things to gather," she stammered.

"Be quick about it. I've got a full day today."

Shocked by his brusqueness, Elizabeth returned to the store, followed by Mr. Cole, who seemed intent on ensuring she would not return to see his mother. "Everything all right?" she asked, but she flinched inwardly. Clearly things were not all right.

Mr. Cole softened slightly. "It's a very busy day. Truly. You're welcome to see my mother on the first of the month as usual."

Elizabeth glanced down at her list for something to do, but her face heated with the slight. Did he think visiting his mother was just a pastime?

Mr. Cole passed around the counter and Elizabeth went in search of the last few items.

Then the bell on the door rang and Mr. and Mrs. Sommers entered.

They spotted her immediately and it took every ounce of Elizabeth's stamina to smile politely.

"We haven't had a chance to congratulate you," said Mrs. Sommers. "Indeed, we've barely seen anyone in your family since we heard of Rose's engagement."

"It's harvest," said Elizabeth. "And it doesn't cease to be our busiest season of the year just because of a few engagements."

Mrs. Sommers blinked and Mr. Sommers smiled stiffly.

"Of course, of course," said Mrs. Sommers. "And we will be at your home, with the rest of the town, this Saturday."

"Lovely," said Elizabeth.

"Will Rose's beau be joining us?"

"No, he'll remain at the coast."

"Oh how very sad for her. Will he be visiting for the holidays?"

"I do not know." Seized with a powerful inclination to be gone from the grocers, and confident her mother could wait on the rest of the items on the list, Elizabeth moved past the Sommers and out the door without taking leave of them.

"Elizabeth!" Elizabeth turned around as Mr. Cole ran toward her. "What was that about?" he demanded.

Incredulous, Elizabeth said, "I don't know it is any concern of yours."

"That was rather rude, wasn't it? Honestly, I've never seen you behave that way."

"I could say the same for you. Whatever is wrong with your mother, you needn't be so harsh."

Mr. Cole grew stern. "Leave my mother out of this."

"It's why you're in such a foul mood, isn't it?"

"Elizabeth, you see my mother once a month. You have no idea what I have to deal with. But of course you don't, I apologize. Please say hello to your family." The final words were ground out as if they cost him a great deal to say. He turned around and went back to the store.

Stunned. Wounded. And with a growing headache, Elizabeth continued her journey home. Mortified at having to explain to her family why she only succeeded in bringing the cheesecloth, she slowed her pace halfway there.

It was quite possibly the worst experience in town she'd ever had.

16

That's Why You Were So Foul at Supper

Elizabeth was still stinging from her trip to the grocers. She'd gone to the kitchen when she returned home, dropped the cheesecloth on the table in front of her mother, and immediately went out the back door into the grounds before anyone could ask her about the missing items.

She hid behind her foul mood at supper so her family would know to leave off inquiring about her trip to town. Allison and Rose kept glancing at her, so she gave them such a withering look that they both stayed silent.

Preferring to go early to bed than relax with her family in the sitting room, Elizabeth disappeared upstairs. Not five minutes after she'd sealed herself inside her room did Rose knock on the door and poke her head in. "Edward Cole awaits you in the sitting room."

Elizabeth felt her face grow hot. The burning continued when she realized Rose had most certainly noticed. "Shall I tell him you'll be down soon?"

"I'll tell him myself," said Elizabeth. Likely he wanted to reprimand her for attempting to see his mother without permission and for her rudeness to the Sommers. While she wasn't entirely proud of her behavior, she would not back down in the face of his hypocrisy. While she might not understand the length of his suffering, *he* did not understand what it was to have an entire town freely make assumptions about your life, and the life of your family, while you must endure it politely for the sake of propriety.

Surely she could choose to be like Allison and meet the attacks head on, or like Samantha and respond with wit and laughter, but the truth was, all Elizabeth had ever wanted was to be seen as a valuable member of society. Her proclaimed beauty had always been her safeguard. She moved in and out of social circles and was always petted and praised when she was in Port Town.

But in Tree Town, she was just one of a pack of other beautiful Hartford sisters who went too long without marriage proposals and whose independence was sure to drive suitors away for all of time.

With the engagements of Allison and Rose, she'd thought they'd be left in peace, but it wasn't enough for the town, and they were now calling for her marriage as if they deserved it.

Elizabeth was almost ready to declare herself a spinster for life, when she entered the parlor to speak with Edward Cole.

He stood in the center of the room, hat in his hands, and he appeared much more the gentle, open Mr. Cole she was accustomed to. "You left your list behind. And your basket. I've returned them, along with the items you were seeking."

"That is very kind. Thank you." Elizabeth walked further into the room. Asking Mr. Cole to sit felt entirely too intimate, so she walked to her piano and stood beside it.

Mr. Cole twisted his hat one loop around. "I wanted to apologize for my rudeness today. My mother was in a bad way, and I took it out on you. I do appreciate you visiting her every month. Whatever your motives, it brightens her day. She's even brighter the whole week leading up to it."

Elizabeth watched Mr. Cole twist his hat again. "I do enjoy seeing her."

"Good."

Elizabeth tilted her head to the side. "You don't believe me?"

Mr. Cole shrugged and studied the hat in his hands.

"You think I'm selfish, don't you?"

He sighed. "It really doesn't matter what I think."

"Well, it's true. I am selfish. But that doesn't mean I don't care for you. And your mother."

"I know that, which is why I'm holding my tongue. I really hope you will continue to visit her."

"Of course I will."

"Thank you."

"Is it really so bad?"

"Yes."

"I am sorry."

"Thank you. Though you'll find me equally selfish in wishing her suffering would end."

"And by its end, your own suffering."

"I bear up well most days. Today was not one of them."

"You're entitled to your share of bad spells."

"I would have preferred to keep it a secret a bit longer. It was unfortunate you had to see me that way."

"Why unfortunate? You're a good, kind soul, Mr. Cole. But you are not required to be perfect." With these words, the tension in the room dissipated. Elizabeth took a seat on the piano bench. "Did you truly come all this way to apologize?"

"Your family has always been good to us. I was grieved I had offended you."

"And your mother? You were able to leave her?"

"She was sleeping soundly when I left. Thankfully, she sleeps well through the night."

"Then will you be able to attend the fires this year, at Harvest?"

Mr. Cole smiled. "Your sister has offered her housekeeper as a caretaker for the day. I'm closing the store and will be present for the whole of Harvest."

"Mr. Cole! That's wonderful. How truly gallant of Mrs. Bishop."

He tossed his hat between his hands. "You know, I keep asking the Hartfords to call me Edward. I really wish you would."

"I believe 'Mr. Cole' has become more endearing than a term of respect—that is—to say—we certainly respect you—it's just, not what you might think—it means." Elizabeth shook her head, confused at why her words were stumbling.

"Ah, well. I'll say no more about it."

Elizabeth recovered herself. Folding her hands, she said, "But your request has been noted, and we will take it into consideration." She finished with her most charming smile.

She could have imagined it, but Edward Cole blushed just a little beneath his receding hairline.

Elizabeth walked Mr. Cole to the door. After he was gone, she proceeded through the hallway, only to encounter Rose, Allison, and Victoria seated on the stairs.

Elizabeth placed her hands on her hips. "What on earth?

"What did Mr. Cole want?" Victoria asked. They leaned forward eagerly.

"It is absolutely none of your business. I am going to bed." Elizabeth tried to thread her way through the maze of sisters on the stairs, but Allison grabbed her knees, Rose grabbed her hips, and Victoria grabbed the rest of her. They tumbled down the stairs in a ball of squeals and laughter until Mrs. Hartford stuck her head over the banister.

"What's all this?" she cried.

"Sorry, Mama!" Rose said.

"Just a bit of exercise before bed," Allison answered.

Mrs. Hartford shook her head of curls and returned to her room.

In a mass of skirts, the sisters surfaced, gasping for breath. "If anyone in the world saw us like this..." Elizabeth said.

"There's no one here to see. It's just us." Allison clipped Elizabeth on the cheek and Elizabeth shoved her hand away.

"No seriously," said Victoria. "Why was Mr. Cole here? He's never out this time of night."

"We said some things to one another today. He wanted to apologize."

"That's why you were so foul at supper," Allison said.

Elizabeth whipped her head toward her older sister. "Was the cheesecloth *your* idea?"

The usually quick-witted Allison was tossed off balance by the direct question. She stammered for a response, which caused Elizabeth to laugh. "You have all let this marriage business go to your heads. I am *not* marrying Edward Cole, so please put it out of your minds." She stood up and climbed the stairs, leaving Allison and Rose gaping at each other.

"Mr. Cole? For Elizabeth?" Victoria said. "He is too old." She stood up and followed Elizabeth.

17

Daniel Copeland is a Fried Cutlet

Elizabeth awoke in the middle of the night from one of the strangest dreams. Her body was flushed, and she threw off the covers and padded to her bureau to light a candle.

Blond hair cascading down her shoulders, she opened a drawer. Inside were notes and small trinkets, little treasures bestowed upon her by her admirers from the coast.

She'd had more suitors than any of her sisters, a fact she was quietly proud of. She kept the tokens of flattery close, to remind herself she could have a match at any moment—if she so desired.

Tossing her hair and snatching up a ribbon to tie it back, her skin was still radiating heat. As she sorted through the little notes, a string of beads, pressed flowers, a broach, and one small book of poetry, she suddenly felt very childish for keeping such things. Smashing them all together, she shoved them back in the drawer and leaned on the bureau as she bit her lip and allowed herself to recall the dream she'd just had.

Her body flushed hotter, for the dream had been highly improper and involved a man she had spoken to earlier that day.

Dear Mr. Edward Cole.

When they were much younger, she and Victoria had giggled behind their hands at the handsome boys who fell over themselves with overtures to any pretty ladies attending a ball at the coast. But they'd never whispered about Edward Cole. To her knowledge, neither had any of her other sisters. He was completely off limits. A breed apart. Not because he was unsuitable, no, but because he was entirely too good for anyone.

Elizabeth placed two fingers on her lips, tracing them lightly. In her dream, Mr. Cole had been a very good—

She stood abruptly and went to the window. She threw it open and let the icy air hit her searing face. The cold was too much to bear for very long, so she closed it again after a few seconds. Once she'd crawled back into bed, she pulled the covers up to her chin.

Then, a wave of sadness rolled in, bringing with it the sting of tears to prick Elizabeth's eyes.

For Elizabeth Hartford had carried a secret for the past four years.

She was in love with Edward Cole.

She'd spent her whole life wanting his approval and vying for his attention, but he had never seen her as anything more than a younger sister.

Once more, he was a grocer. And beneath the Hartfords' class. While her sisters did not care about such things, Elizabeth always had, imagining she'd marry a wealthy, fashionable man. Perhaps a politician or an aristocrat. It was what everyone in town expected from her.

It was an improbable match, and Elizabeth had resolved to give up the childish fantasy for good.

Then—the dream.

She shimmied down beneath the sheets and again recalled the scandalous dream. It brought a smile, which quickly disappeared in a haze of despair.

If she desired, she could have a match at any moment.

But there was a very good chance the match she actually wanted was far out of reach.

In the early morning on Harvest Day, Alma Burros arrived at the kitchen of Loretta Humphrey. Aunt Letty was boiling water for tea and offered a cup to Alma, after Alma had invited herself in and sat at the kitchen table.

After a brief pause (she allowed sufficient time for Loretta Humphrey to inquire into the reason for her visit, but when the inquiry was not forthcoming, she proceeded on), Alma said, "Do you know who's already arrived at the Hartford Estate?"

"Who?" Aunt Letty asked.

"Daniel Copeland! Upon my life, every year he shows after the work is done. This year, he was one of the firsts, second only to the family and Edward Cole. What do you think it means?"

"It means he intends to help this year. And, might I ask, why are you on your way so early?"

"I'm always up and about early. You know me. Don't like to sit still. It should be rather interesting this year. Last year, not a single Hartford sister had any prospects or attachments. This year, one is married and two are engaged. Who would have ever guessed the fortune of the family could change so quickly? I do wish Rose's beau were here, though. We haven't had a chance to get to know anything about him. I hear he's part Italian, that would explain why he is so dark and handsome. But the Italians have been known for their loose living. I do hope their father was a harsh critic, but knowing Mr. Hartford, he probably let Rose choose for herself. He always gave those girls far too much freedom, if you ask me. It is quite uncivilized. And that Allison—she's positively wild."

Loretta Humphrey blinked over the top of her teacup at Alma Burros, who didn't seem to remember Allison was engaged to her nephew.

"I say," she continued. "I don't believe Daniel Copeland ever worked a full day in his life." Alma Burros strummed her fingers on the table. "Aha!" She threw a hand into the air. "He's hoping to marry one of the daughters. I'm sure it's Elizabeth. He's likely receiving pressure from that old coot to produce an heir and Elizabeth would ensure the offspring was suitably attractive."

"Alma Burros, your imagination is quite fanciful."

"It would greatly improve the prospects of the

Hartfords. Copelands and Hartfords are the finest families in our county. An alliance is just what this town needs."

Loretta Humphrey opened her mouth to speak, then decided against it. The best way to deal with Alma Burros was to let her have her say. Once she'd finished, she'd clear off and find a new victim.

Alma eventually did become bored with her unenthusiastic listener and took her leave. Off to the wheat fields she went, in search of a party of Hartfords. There she felt sure to catch a glimpse of Daniel Copeland.

Allison was high up in a wagon, tying down sheaves of wheat, when she spotted Alma coming in the direction of their working party. She instinctively looked around for anything out of sort that might be unhealthy for Alma to see. Scanning the fields, her eyes landed on Daniel, who was aiding Mr. Cole in tying off some already cut bundles. She sighed and shook her head. Daniel Copeland never came early to Harvest. Rose and Allison suspected he was there to keep an eye on things and ensure no matchmaking was afoot.

Mr. Cole had also arrived early, with a spring in his step. Rose and Allison agreed he could have just been happy for his freedom from the store and a reprieve from his mother, but this did not keep them from watching for signs of affection between him and Elizabeth.

There were none.

Just the usual brotherly-sister cordiality.

In fact, nothing at all seemed to have changed between them since the other night.

Rose and Allison resigned to give up the scheme. If they hadn't fallen in love yet, there was nothing more to be done.

"What is it?" Ethan asked. He'd looked up when he heard Allison sigh.

"Alma Burros on her way to see our new friend hard at work."

Ethan handed her a reel of twine. "What new friend?"

"Daniel Copeland."

"Oh." Ethan looked in the direction of Daniel and Mr. Cole.

Allison remembered Daniel and Ethan working together during harvest when they were young boys. They were nearing their teen years when Daniel stopped coming around. Allison had always assumed the other boy had grown allergic to hard work. "Do you remember that one Harvest Day when you and Daniel got into a fight?"

"Yes." Ethan smiled. "He started it, but I was the one who was punished."

"I recall it was you who started it."

"Whatever the reason, it was a good one. And that was probably the only thrashing he ever got."

"I hope not. Boys need lots of thrashings." Allison began to get off the wagon. Ethan held out a gloved hand to help her down.

"Well I hope you'll be good for it," Ethan said. "If we have any boys."

"What if we have girls?"

"I like girls, too. I had lots of sisters, remember?"

"No bad memories?"

"No bad memories." Ethan kissed her against the side of the cart.

"Hello there," William announced his approach with Samantha. "Please continue enjoying yourselves. Just move out of the way, the rest of us are trying to work."

It was just the time when the rest of the town began to arrive. Wagons of townsfolk—Dr. and Mrs. Vaughn, Mr. and Mrs. Sommers, Mr. Winnifred (the rector) and his wife—rolled up to the estate. The number of young people had dwindled considerably over the years as children did what they were born to do: marry and have children of their own. Most had moved away to Port Town or other nearby counties.

More and more people arrived throughout the morning, and Samantha remarked to her husband that, while the turnout was usually large, this year was very large indeed. "I think most of the town must be here. I don't believe many are missing." They made their way to the table spread with the midday meal. Victoria and Elizabeth were assisting Mrs. Hartford, and were joined by most of the wives in preparing food for the workers.

Samantha spotted Daniel, resting against the side of a wagon. She retrieved an extra sandwich and approached him, extending the sandwich as she drew near. "Hungry?"

He accepted the gift with a dipping, sardonic smile. "I was just thinking it's a pity there are so few young people left in town. How will Elizabeth and Victoria find husbands?"

Samantha never thought she'd feel relieved to hear his cynical tone. She relaxed and leaned against the wagon beside him. "I have yet to apologize for the unkind things I said in the grocers last month. I hope you can forgive me and we can be friends again."

Daniel squinted at her out of the corner of his eye. "You're apologizing to *me*? I dare say I deserved whatever you said, though I don't remember the details."

"Don't you?"

"Well, I suppose I do recall the conversation. I recall behaving like a fool and making you very angry. The fault was all mine."

"That is very gallant of you to say. And I forgive you."

Daniel shifted from one foot to the other and wondered if he should say, "thank you." He decided to shrug it off and ask, "So, what are your plans for the youngest Hartford sisters?"

"Honestly, I hadn't thought much on it. We've been away half the month."

"Oh yes. How was the coast?"

"Beautiful, this time of year. And cold. We looked for a house."

"You're moving?"

"Not just yet, but we're making plans. We—" but she was cut off by Elizabeth calling for her to help pass out the rest of the sandwiches.

As the day wore on, spirits rose. Nearing sundown, the final stores were being laid away and pyres were prepared for lighting the moment the sun set, signaling the end of Harvest Day. Mr. Winnifred tuned his fiddle, and Mr. Sommers prepped the strings on his guitar. The townsfolk gathered, shoulder to shoulder, to watch the final sliver of sun sink behind the trees. The moment it disappeared, a cheer arose, followed by applause. The music began, and the Tree Town residents began to kick up their feet. Very soon the dancing was well underway.

Harvest Day was livelier than usual. Elizabeth found the energy quite intoxicating. Perhaps it was the addition of William to the party as well as the returned Ethan. Dear Reuben had to miss the festivities, but Rose was glowing, anyway, and the entire town seemed to have turned out for the whole of the day. There were even a few faces who rarely came for the working part of the day, Daniel Copeland being one of them.

She had a suspicion he was up to something, but she couldn't figure out what. It almost felt like he'd come to keep an eye on them. His eyes followed her and Victoria and the other Hartfords like he was hoping to catch them at something. He'd always been severe on the Hartford sisters, waiting to pounce at any opportunity to ridicule them. But this watchfulness had a different flavor.

Mr. Cole had come at first light, but Elizabeth did not find herself anywhere near him until just before the fires were lit. She wasn't avoiding him on purpose (at least she didn't think so). Once or twice she felt him glance in her direction, but he did not seek her out. This bothered her. It bothered her almost as much as the fact she hadn't had a chance to speak to him all day.

While she was unsure if she or Mr. Cole were deliberately circling wide of the other, she was, to her chagrin, deeply aware she was paying attention to Mr. Cole and her own proximity to him.

And this *really* bothered her.

As the cheers subsided once the sun had dipped beneath the edge of the horizon, Mr. Cole suddenly appeared beside her. She did not remember moving near him, so it meant he must have moved near her.

Elizabeth's body began tingling with anticipation.

He turned toward her, grinning in a very boyish, uninhibited way. "This might be one of the best days I've had in a long time."

Considering he was covered in the evidence of hard labor in the fields, Elizabeth gathered he was referring to the reprieve from caring for his mother. "I'm glad to hear it. You deserve it," she responded.

Mr. Cole's smile softened. He shoved his hands in his pockets, an action common for a younger man. But then again, Mr. Cole was a young man still, though many were inclined to view him as much older.

He was, in fact, only two years older than Reuben and William. Not very old at all.

Mr. Cole settled back on his heels, quite at ease. "You know my secret, now," he said. "I'm glad of it. I never would have told you voluntarily."

For lack of something to do with her hands, Elizabeth began bunching a bit of her skirt in her fists. "Why was it such a secret?" she asked. "We all know it can't be easy."

"And because of it, you all saw me as a saint. I had not realized what a burden *that* was."

"You don't like being revered as a saint?" Elizabeth teased.

The pyre near them was set ablaze and Elizabeth felt the heat of it overwhelm them. She took a step away and Mr. Cole remained beside her as she walked.

"Sainthood is not at all what people think it is," said Mr. Cole.

"And what do people think it is?"

Mr. Cole shrugged. "No idea. But I'll gather research and report back."

"I thought you might have first-hand experience to impart."

Mr. Cole chuckled. "Like you said the other night, I'm only human and not required to be perfect *all* the time."

Elizabeth flushed a little. Did he remember everything she said? She recovered quickly. "Right. You must only be perfect during the week. And on Sundays, of course."

"I'm afraid I'm going to need a little more time for imperfections."

"Fine then. You pick the day. Any day you want. On that day, you're allowed to shed your saintly-ness and be a regular flawed human like the rest of us."

Mr. Cole was silent a moment. They'd reached the edge of the woods. Elizabeth had not realized they'd walked so far. The light of the moon began to replace the light of day, and she was about to suggest they turn back when Mr. Cole looked at her. Something in his eyes reminded her of the dream she'd had the other night, and she was glad the light was so dim so he would not see how her face was burning. "Today," he said. "I choose today."

Elizabeth changed her mind about turning back. Together, they entered the woods.

The night was full of laughter, dancing, music. William was enthralled, as he'd never seen anything like it. "This is the one time of year no one criticizes the Hartfords for their queer ways," Samantha explained. "Everyone is having too much fun to criticize."

Hours of dancing continued, and soon Samantha and William took a break near one of the fires. They were just sitting down on a quilt, when they spotted Allison standing beside a wagon, beckoning them furiously with flailing arms.

"What can that be about?" William wondered.

"We better go," Samantha said, climbing to her feet. "Alma Burros might have fallen into a trough."

When they arrived, Ethan and Rose were already waiting with Allison while she paced excitedly. "Guess what I just saw," she blurted out. "Our proper, never-be-alone-with-a-man-without-a-chaperone Elizabeth is, at this moment, walking *alone* with Mr. Cole in the woods."

Ethan covered his mouth (a mouth that was grinning broadly).

Rose clapped her hands.

Samantha suppressed a squeal, while taking hold of William's sleeve.

"What are they doing? What are they saying?"

William asked.

"I *could* have stayed to eavesdrop, but instead I ran over here to tell all of you." Allison straightened, waiting for her family to praise her.

"You *left* them all alone?"

"I was never with them. I just happened to be resting by the brook when I heard voices. Naturally I hid, when I saw who it was, and snuck back here as quickly as I could."

Samantha shook William's sleeve. "We thought it was off, but looks like it's very much on."

"Mr. Cole is far too much of a gentleman to behave like this unless he truly cares for her."

"And Elizabeth would never behave so unless her feelings ran very deep," Rose concurred.

Allison cheered, "Daniel Copeland is a fried cutlet." The others quieted her.

"So? What do we do now?" asked Ethan. (Matchmaking was very new to him.)

"We wait," said Samantha. "They don't seem to need any help from us."

"I would like to take full credit for this match," said Allison. "If I hadn't thought of the cheesecloth, neither of them would have recognized their true feelings."

"They're not engaged yet," Rose cautioned.

"But it won't be long now. Let's return to the fire before anyone notices we're all together." She took hold of Ethan's arm and one by one they tiptoed back out amongst the very lively Tree Town residents.

The festivities of Harvest Day often lasted late, sometimes until dawn. For this reason, William and Samantha had prepared to stay the night at the

Hartford estate, thus ensuring Samantha wouldn't have to wait to hear the details about Elizabeth and Mr. Cole's midnight stroll through the woods.

When the last of the guests had departed, the family returned to the house. Mrs. Hartford had gone to bed hours earlier, but none of the sisters would sleep until they'd heard from Elizabeth.

In Allison's room, they crawled up on the bed or spread out on the floor. It'd been months since they'd all been under the same roof, and Samantha beamed at her four younger sisters as Victoria ducked under her arm and they all laughed over the evening, agreeing it was one of the best Harvest Day's in memory.

"There is one memory of this day I will never forget," Allison said, turning her head dramatically in Elizabeth's direction.

"Shh," Rose hissed sharply. "Let her tell us in her own time."

"Tell us what? What's going on?" Victoria asked.

"Oh well, it's not a secret now," said Samantha. She turned to Elizabeth. "How was your walk with Mr. Cole?" The other sisters grinned widely when Elizabeth turned pink.

"Heavens," she cried. "Can't I do anything in this town without scrutiny?"

"No, those have never been the rules," Allison declared.

"It was *just* a walk. Mr. Cole has always been a friend and we needn't run away with fantasies. Goodness, you really are all intoxicated with this marriage business. Haven't we been brought up to *not* be like other girls and let the thoughts of matrimony carry us away until we've lost all our senses?"

Allison propped her chin on her fist. "While I love your tactics of deflection, we'd really love to know what transpired."

"How do you feel?" asked Rose. "And did Mr. Cole express what he feels?"

"Feels about what?" Elizabeth tossed her hands in the air. "Are none of you listening?"

"Oh, we're all ears," Allison said.

"Elizabeth," said Samantha gently. "It isn't like you or Mr. Cole to disappear into the woods—alone. However, if you tell us it was nothing more than a walk between friends, then we will believe you and say no more." She gave Rose and Allison a pointed look.

Elizabeth straightened and pursed her lips. She was silent a long moment. The moment dragged on just a little too long and ended when Allison threw her fist into the air. "I knew it! Are you engaged?"

"No," Elizabeth said quietly, her very pink face and small smile betraying her feelings.

Rose scooted off the bed and took Elizabeth's hands in her own. "What did he say? What did you say? And then what did he say back?"

Elizabeth's smile grew larger. "It's all so strange. I'm not even sure how it happened. Is this how it was for you all? One minute you would never be anything more than friends and the next, you feel like the happiest person in the world?"

"It changed suddenly for me," said Allison.

"I think I loved Reuben for some time before I knew

I loved him," said Rose.

"I began corresponding with William to see if we'd be a good match, before we fell in love, but I was certainly looking for it." Samantha sighed.

Elizabeth sighed also. "Mr. Cole is so good and so kind. Did you know he wanted to be a teacher, before his father died and his mother took ill?"

"How very tragic," said Allison. "We were all barred from professions because we are female. Mr. Cole was trapped because of circumstances. I never thought for a moment he had any ambitions beyond the store."

"Because he never complains." Elizabeth hugged a pillow to her chest. "After the other day, he is more comfortable sharing his deepest feelings with me."

"Did he share any other feelings?" Allison smirked, then cried, "Ouch!" when Rose pinched her.

"Not specifically. I think he'd speak to Father, first. But I could tell he felt what I felt, perhaps even more deeply."

"Did he say if he was going to speak to Father?" asked Allison.

"No, but honestly, I'm in no hurry. There's so much going on these days. And his mother is very sick. He did not say, but I think it is very likely she will not make it to Christmas."

"Oh my," said Samantha. "I did not know it was so very bad."

The sisterly tête-à-tête sobered in the aftermath of this revelation. Though Allison was very sad to hear of Mrs. Cole's condition, she thought it was just like Elizabeth to sap all the joy out of a situation and remind them of the frailty of life. "What a wonderful time for Mr. Cole to begin an attachment," said Allison. "I'm sure you will be a comfort to him."

Elizabeth folded her hands. "I do hope to be a comfort to him, come what may."

"I meant a different sort of comfort, but all right."

The four sisters began pummeling Allison with pillows.

18

The Race isn't Over Yet

On Sunday morning, Samantha communicated slight disappointment to William. "It is one thing if Elizabeth and Mr. Cole did not love one another. But to know they do, and there will likely be no engagement this year is a cruel blow. We are so close, but I don't suppose it counts in the game if they are not officially engaged."

"Perhaps we could inquire of Daniel if this would be allowed."

"You know he won't agree."

"We might need to speak with him anyway. Did you know he took Victoria riding?"

"What? She never said anything to me."

"I don't like it."

"It's just Daniel."

"But you know what he's trying to do, don't you?"

"Of course. He's trying to keep her busy and distracted so she won't have time to think of marriage. He has a vested interest in *not* becoming attached to her."

"I don't have any fear of that. My fear is for her. He's using her, and she doesn't know it."

Samantha pinched her lips together. "Perhaps. Perhaps we should invite Daniel to tea?"

"I'll ask him next chance I get."

On the Monday following Harvest Day, Daniel arrived at the field on time. As usual, Victoria was seated on the fence, waiting for him.

"No Elizabeth?" he began.

"She's with—oh never mind. It's just me."

Not entirely disappointed at the loss of Elizabeth's company, he said, "I was thinking, I have this mare in our stables. She's very gentle and doesn't get much riding time. Would you—be interested in giving her a try?"

"Why Daniel, you didn't say anything about her before."

"I wanted to be sure you'd stick with it." He rode up along the fence and helped Victoria climb onto Ebony behind him. Her arms circled around him and Daniel, quite suddenly, felt very strong.

"I'd love to ride her. Are you sure it'd be all right?" Victoria held on as they cantered down the trail that led to the stables.

"I'm sure. She needs exercise. You'll be perfect for her."

They arrived at the grand Copeland stables. In the center stall was a soft, golden mare, a good bit smaller than Ebony. It came to the gate and hung its head over, as if it were expecting Victoria.

"She's beautiful," said Victoria. She dismounted and went directly to the mare. "What's her name?"

Daniel cleared his throat. "I—um—she doesn't have a name."

"No name? How long have you had her?"

Daniel shrugged. "Not long."

"She needs a name."

"Very well. You name her."

"You want me to name her?"

"Of course, whatever you like."

"I'll have to think about it. It needs to be perfect. Maybe after I ride her I'll be able to think of something."

For the first time, Victoria rode alone. When Ebony began to move forward, the mare followed. Victoria, thrilled to be riding by herself, kept squealing with delight. Every time she did, Daniel looked over his shoulder, afraid she'd startle the mare. But the horse didn't seem to mind and patiently followed along.

Victoria loosened the reins and relaxed in the saddle. "You're such a good teacher, Daniel. Look at me now. You'd never suspect that a month ago I'd barely ever ridden at all."

"Yes, you seem very comfortable." Daniel was grateful her horse was positioned slightly behind his so she wouldn't know he blushed at the compliment.

Victoria chatted away, asking questions about this brook, or that tree, or where Daniel liked to explore as a child.

Daniel wanted to ask her something, to begin a conversation on his own, but he felt just as unsure about that as Victoria had felt on her first ride.

How does one begin a normal conversation when sarcasm has been one's habitual means of communication?

Once they arrived back at the stables, Victoria didn't wait for Daniel to help her down, but dismounted gracefully by herself. She pulled the reins over the mare's head just as she had seen Daniel do many times.

"Angel," Victoria said.

"Beg pardon?" said Daniel.

"I think her name is Angel. What do you think?" Victoria looked at Daniel with earnest sincerity.

"I—it's—it's perfect," said Daniel.

"Really?" Victoria was delighted. Without warning, she hugged Daniel and said, "Thank you, Daniel. This was one of the best days I've ever had."

Daniel, as usual when interacting with Victoria, didn't know how to interact.

He cleared his throat and said, "It was only riding," and turned away to give instructions to one of the grooms.

Daniel walked with Victoria toward the house with the intent of taking her down the drive back to the road. When they came into view of the Copeland mansion, Victoria exclaimed, "What an enormous house. Is it yours?"

Daniel shrugged. "It's my mother's."

"Then where do you live?" Victoria smiled at him teasingly.

Daniel only shrugged again and began the walk down the drive.

"May I see it sometime?" asked Victoria innocently.

"Of course," said Daniel.

Nothing else was said until goodbye when they reached the road. Daniel tromped back up the drive, shaking his head and wondering how a small woman like Victoria could be so intimidating.

"Daniel Copeland, you haven't been to visit us in a very long time." William and Samantha hailed Daniel as he sauntered down Main Street.

"Perhaps because you haven't provided an opportunity. There hasn't been a match made in the Hartford family in over a month." Daniel halted and waited for them to come closer.

"Would an invitation provide a good opportunity?" asked Samantha.

"If an invitation were offered, I might be inclined to accept. What would be the occasion?"

"The occasion of simply having nothing to do on this very fine evening," said William.

Daniel looked slyly at the couple standing before him. "Don't tell me," he said. "Romance soon dies and you are now looking for diversion?"

Almost imperceptibly, Samantha flinched. And Daniel witnessed William's jaw tighten.

"We are quite content with one another," said Samantha. "But we have no engagements this evening and we've been seeking an opportunity to visit with you. Would you join us for coffee at our home?"

Daniel shoved his hands in his pockets and shook his head. "Regrettably, my mother worries when I stay out too late. Perhaps another time?" He brushed past them, retracing his steps back to the Copeland estate.

Daniel simmered during his walk home. Instead of going into the house, he went into the woods, where he found a good log to sit on. Maybe he was going mad, but ever since his head-to-head with Samantha, that dreadful day in the grocers, he'd suddenly become aware of other peoples' reactions to him. He was having difficulty understanding this new element to his life, and he was sure he did not like it.

He'd never realized how people tolerated him with simple indifference. As it were, he knew he had no one to blame but himself. He'd created an idle, cynical reputation for himself, and had become quite comfortable with it. It never occurred to him that someone might truly take offense, not until he had provoked Samantha (who happened to be one of few people he genuinely admired—though he'd never admit it to anyone).

They'd spoken about their tiff since, and she'd forgiven him, but instead of trying to undo the damage, he only succeeded in making it worse. Maybe he was a dunce, and deserved to be kept at a distance.

The next day, Daniel found himself standing in front of Samantha and William's house. He hesitated before approaching the door and knocking. What was there to be afraid of? It was only William and Samantha. Up to the door he went, and rapped only a few times, silently hoping that no one was home.

The door was opened by the old woman—Daniel could never remember her name—and he was admitted. The old woman announced him in the parlor, where Samantha sat with her embroidery. These Temples were becoming high society. The only other person he knew who had her guests announced was his own mother.

Samantha looked up and smiled, but it lacked its usual warmth. "Come in, Daniel," she said.

Daniel leaned against the door and watched her thoughtfully before clearing his throat. "I thought perhaps I might call on you and William sometime this week?"

Samantha tilted her head to the side. "Are you making an appointment?"

He shrugged.

Samantha glanced at the clock on the mantel. "It's almost time for tea. William will be breaking soon. Would you like to join us?"

Daniel slowly nodded, wishing he hadn't come. He sat uncomfortably in a chair across from Samantha, while she attempted to make small talk.

"I hear you and Tori have been riding together," she said.

"Yes, we have."

"How is it coming?"

"How is what coming?"

"The riding lessons. She said you were teaching her." Samantha turned her embroidery loop over and tied a knot where she had left off.

"Well, sort of. I'm not much of a teacher."

Samantha jerked the thread and snapped it, but

continued staring at her work instead of putting it away. She toyed with it aimlessly and stared about the room, as if in search of another topic for conversation.

Daniel leaned forward. "I thought you'd forgiven me?" he said.

Samantha looked back at him. She sighed and relaxed. "I have. I'm sorry. I'm just concerned, that's all."

"Concerned about what?"

"About you."

"What for?"

Samantha stared at her lap again. "I think you do not realize you have the power to hurt others."

Daniel fidgeted. "Samantha, we're friends. I'd hate to think that—there were—things between us. Is there anything I can do to make it not so?"

Samantha smiled genuinely. "Yes, there is something you can do. I want you to come take tea with us once a week. Whether you feel like it or not, whether there's an occasion or not, we want to see more of you."

"We?"

"Yes, William and I."

"Are you sure about that?"

"Yes, she is sure," said a voice from the entryway. Daniel turned toward it as William came forward and took a seat next to Samantha. "We extend the invitation together. We aren't going to be making our home in Tree Town much longer and we want to be better friends before we leave."

Daniel sat forward. "I've been meaning to talk to you about that. Samantha mentioned something about you moving. What's that all about?"

"Accept the invitation and then we'll tell you."

"Yes, yes, I accept."

"Very good. The past year, my duties in Port Town have not been heavy because of my marriage to Samantha. At the beginning of the New Year, my father is turning the management of the shipping yard completely over to me. My frequent visits to the coast have been for my slow accommodation into the business. So the first week in January, we will completely relocate to Port Town."

"Rose will be there, won't she?" Daniel asked.

Samantha's eyes brightened a bit. "Yes, I'm trying to persuade Reuben to purchase a house near ours. It will greatly comfort me to know one of my sisters is nearby."

"Well then, I congratulate you both. And look on the bright side, when you come home for visits you'll be able to stay in your parents' home instead of a mile away in town."

"That's what I've been telling Samantha."

"And when their home is bursting at the seams with men and babies, our home is too full of unused rooms. Feel free to overflow to it. It's much closer than town anyway."

"Thank you, Daniel," said William.

"That is very kind of you," said Samantha.

"Now for another matter." William leaned forward and looked Daniel squarely in the face. "In your eyes, is the game still on?"

Daniel chuckled. "Of course it is. You still have two more sisters to match up."

"And one of those sisters has been your riding companion as of late?"

"If you are referring to Victoria, then yes, we have been riding together."

"With any ulterior motives?"

Daniel smirked. "And if there were?"

"What are they?"

"Why should I tell you? You might sabotage my plans."

"Then there are ulterior motives?"

"I didn't say that."

"This does concern our little sister and we want to know what you are planning."

Daniel suddenly realized that William and Samantha were quite serious.

Finally, with a sincerity equal to their own, he said, "You don't have to worry. Even if I were capable of tampering with Victoria's heart, I wouldn't."

"Is that a promise?"

"Yes."

"Then what is your plan?"

Daniel shook his head. "All right," he said. "You were both open with me about your plans for your sisters and I had the freedom to criticize them to my heart's content. Now I suppose it's time for me to take my own medicine.

"I do have a plan. The plan is to keep Victoria busy and away from home so that she won't be interested in thinking about marriage. That is all. So far, she has learned to ride a horse, something she always wanted. Even I enjoy myself from time to time. It's perfectly harmless and fills some of the very dull hours of my day with a little amusement. So long as she is enjoying herself, I plan for it to continue until the New Year has come and I have successfully won our challenge."

In Daniel's opinion, William's smile of relief was a long time in coming. But it came. He let out a sigh and sat back easily on the sofa.

"Aren't you worried Victoria will be disappointed when she realizes you're using her to win a bet?" Samantha asked.

Daniel hadn't thought of this, and made no reply.

"Well then," said William "I suppose Samantha and I better get busy if we're going to win."

"Don't be too hard on yourselves. You've done very well. No one would have ever believed it possible for three sisters to become engaged in one year. If you lose with more than half the Hartford sisters married, don't forget to congratulate yourselves for your success. That being the case, I wish to raise the stakes."

Both Samantha and William blinked with astonishment. "To what?" asked William.

"I have in mind something related to an admittal of defeat."

"Which means?"

"At the New Year's Eve celebration, the losing party has to proclaim publicly their defeat and acknowledge the winner. That is all."

It was William's turn to chuckle. "Why would we accept such a proposal? Really, Copeland, Samantha and I already bear all the burden of this challenge."

Daniel remained silent, waiting for their resignation. If they refused the raising of the stakes, it foretold they knew, without much doubt, that the race was as good as lost.

In that moment, he locked eyes with Samantha. He could have sworn she was about to decline, but something shifted at just the last minute and she said, "We accept."

William blanched.

"But what if we win? Did you think of that?" Samantha asked.

"You don't really think you're going to, do you?" asked Daniel.

Samantha smiled. "We might just have some luck left."

"But if we do lose," William addressed Samantha. "Would you be willing to stand up in front of all those people and tell them the whole story, exposing your family to ridicule?"

Samantha gave a nervous laugh. "Honestly, Daniel will get the worst of it because Tori will discover her riding partner was swindling her." Samantha gave Daniel a look that warned him to be careful.

"Then you accept?" Daniel strummed his fingers on the arm of his chair.

Samantha and William looked at each other.

"It would be a laugh," said William. "To see Daniel admitting to the entire town that he was the loser and proclaiming you and I the victors."

Daniel rolled his eyes.

"Very well, Daniel. We accept, but don't get too cocky. You haven't won yet."

There was something about William's smile that made Daniel uneasy. "Do you have men in mind for the younger Hartfords?" he asked.

"Let's just say, the race is not over yet."

During tea, Samantha, William, and Daniel were in jovial moods. They talked over the details of William's job and Samantha had the opportunity to express how proud she was of her husband, even if the advancement meant leaving her family behind.

On his way home that evening, Daniel whistled cheerfully. Only when he reached the front steps of the house did he realize he'd stayed so long at the Temple's, he'd forgotten his appointment with Victoria.

19

Must I Be Formal Around You?

First thing the next morning, Daniel scrawled out a note and dispatched it with one of the servants who was on his way to town. He then dressed and went to the stables, where he made himself busy, afraid his note would not be received well and Victoria would never return again.

Nearing noontime, Victoria appeared at the stables. As soon as Daniel looked up and saw her smiling, he breathed a sigh of relief. "You got my note?"

"Yes, and you shouldn't have been so hard on yourself. You should not have forgotten about me, but I actually had a jolly time."

"You did?"

"Yes. I waited for you for half an hour. When you didn't show, I went to the house to inquire after you. I was admitted to your mother—I don't think she's spoken a single word to me my entire life—and she invited me to tea."

Daniel's mouth went dry.

Victoria giggled. "Why are you so shocked? I've always been afraid of your mother, but we had a wonderful time. She asked me to play the piano for her. I tried to get out of it for I know I don't play well. It turns out I've always been comparing myself to Elizabeth, who is extremely talented. But since your mother has never heard Elizabeth play, she was actually quite impressed. I don't think she's the sort of soul who would pay a compliment if she didn't mean it. And, she told me something about you."

Daniel braced himself for whatever heinous story his mother could have inflicted upon this poor, innocent girl.

"She told me you also play the piano."

Daniel shook his head. "I play very ill."

"That isn't what she said. She seemed very proud of your playing."

"Like you, I fear I've always compared myself to my betters."

"Well I insist that you play for me sometime. I won't care what you play. You will, won't you?"

"Of course I will, but you must promise to play for me."

"It's a promise. We'll have our own little concert to entertain your mother."

Daniel had had the horses saddled and ready to depart when Victoria arrived. They were on their way quickly and made the ride a good, long one to make up for the missed engagement of the previous day. As they headed back to the stables, Victoria pulled her horse up beside Daniel's. "I forgot to ask," she said.

"Where were you yesterday? It's none of my business, but I am curious."

"I was visiting with William and Samantha."

"Oh really? Do you visit them often?"

"Just sometimes."

"I'm glad to know that. I didn't think they approved when I told them I was riding with you."

"They weren't exactly pleased when we discussed it yesterday. But I put their minds at ease about it, don't worry."

"Why weren't they pleased? You are all friends after all?"

Daniel bit his lip. The real reason had to do with the wager. "Er—because—you know—no chaperone, and all. But, they had no concerns when I departed, I assure you."

He breathed a sigh of relief when Victoria did not inquire further.

The following day, when Daniel awoke, he saw a light mist coming down. He knew he'd better make preparations should Victoria still come. He didn't think she would turn up, but she did. At her usual time, she entered the stables with a wrap over her head and around her shoulders.

The stables smelled musty from the damp air. Victoria took a seat on a barrel and seemed deep in thought. Daniel stopped grooming Ebony and took a seat on a barrel next to Victoria's.

"Daniel, why is it that no one is clamoring for you to get married?"

"I beg your pardon?"

"I can't remember a time when people did not care

whether we were married or not. My sisters were always asked about their prospects. I believe Samantha didn't have a moment's peace since she turned sixteen! Then people began to say we were too wild or too headstrong or too intelligent and we had better quiet down or no man with any stature would want a wife like a Hartford. And they seemed to think it a terrible failure. But," She turned to face Daniel. "I don't remember anyone ever worrying if *you* would marry. And Mr. Cole has been single as far as I can tell, his whole life. No one seemed bent on finding a wife for *him*, the way they always seemed to want husbands for us. Does not that seem strange?"

Daniel stared into Victoria's very open and honest face and wondered how she could have grown up in such a home and escaped learning the intricate weavings of the world. He shrugged a conceding shoulder. "I suppose a woman's lot has always been quite different than a man's."

Victoria tossed her head. "It's very unfair, don't you think?"

"I suppose it is."

"My sisters have always been happy without husbands. Now all they think about is marriage and matches. I think I shall not get married. I think I shall protest the very institution."

Daniel tipped his hat. "On this venture, I intend to support you."

Rain was pouring fiercely, so Daniel offered to show her the house. They ran through the downpour to the shallow door that led to the conservatory. When Victoria sucked in her breath at the sight, Daniel's heart swelled with satisfaction.

Though the Copelands hardly had any guests, his mother paid particular attention to the maintenance of the fountain and small gardens inside the glass walls. The clinking of the rain on the glass ceiling and the bubbling of the fountain in the center almost made it feel as if they were walking inside a waterfall.

"It's enchanting," Victoria purred. She circled round and round, observing everything.

By and by, Daniel took a seat on one of the stone benches. Once she had walked to one end and back, made a circle around the fountain, and smelled a few of the dwindling roses, she sat next to him and stared ahead.

"Thank you Daniel," she said. "This is beautiful. I needed a change of scenery."

Daniel wished he could say something witty to make her laugh. While deep in concentration, trying to think of just the right thing, he became aware of Victoria leaning against his arm. He stood abruptly. "Shall we explore some more of the house?"

Victoria nodded.

"I must warn you," he said. "There are some places I haven't been in years. I have no idea what we'll find."

"It'll be an adventure," she said, excitement dancing in her eyes.

"Off we go then."

"And we barely finished the second floor." At supper that evening, Victoria was animatedly relating the events of the day to her family. "The third floor is the servants' quarters, and there's a really big attic that Daniel says he's never been in. And we still have to explore the cellar. Daniel says it's been a long time since he's been in certain places in his house."

"When are you going to explore these places?" Mr. Hartford asked. He was the only family member enthusiastically listening.

"On the next rainy day," said Victoria. "I've never been in a house that big. It's like a castle. They have servants all over the place. Though I believe the only reason they have them is to keep the house clean. Daniel is never at home and Mrs. Copeland always sits in her parlor sewing and writing letters, at least that is what Daniel said."

"It's true that Daniel is never at home," said Elizabeth. "I think every time I go to town he is there, wandering about aimlessly."

"But he hasn't been there in a while," said Victoria. "At least, not any day this week."

At this, Allison raised her eyes to look at Rose. Rose reflected Allison's alarm. "When did you begin these riding lessons with Daniel?" she asked Victoria.

"Officially, I suppose just after Harvest Day."

Allison and Rose both glanced in Elizabeth's direction. Elizabeth was fiddling with the food on her plate, absorbed in some thought they could only presume involved Mr. Cole.

Victoria noticed the reaction of her sisters to something she had said. All at once, her smile disappeared.

"And what else did you do this afternoon?" Mr.

Hartford asked Victoria.

"Nothing else," she responded, and she began to eat her meal in silence.

Daniel sat at the grand dining table, across from his mother. At her request, he ate supper with her once a week. All other times he preferred to have it served in his room. His meals with her were quite dull, filled with her prattling on about how she wished he'd improve his life. Most of the time he was able to drown out her voice with his own thoughts, timing his grunts and nods perfectly so that she had no idea he wasn't paying attention.

Tonight was different. She was silent for the first course, and the second. Daniel grew uneasy and found himself wishing she would start chiding him like she usually did. The silence was almost unbearable.

As the main course was served, Mrs. Copeland finally spoke. "I'd like you to bring that Victoria girl to tea sometime."

Daniel almost choked on his veal. "What did you say?" he asked in disbelief.

"I like her. She's very spirited and gave my day a little sunshine. Of course, I won't torture you to remain and take tea with us, but perhaps you could ride in the morning one day this week and she could be my guest for tea."

Daniel wanted to blurt out something about how Victoria couldn't possibly enjoy tea with a bitter old woman, but he knew it would be a lie. Victoria had, for some odd reason, enjoyed her time with his mother. And somehow, he knew she'd rise to the occasion.

"You might consider sending her an invitation," Daniel found himself saying. "I'm supposed to visit William and Samantha on Tuesday afternoon. Perhaps that would be a good time."

"I shall. I'm sure she is unused to receiving invitations. It will be a good experience for her. And it is formally 'the Temples' not 'William and Samantha.'"

"Must I be formal around you, Mother?" Daniel yawned and stretched his arms widely in a way he knew irked her.

"If you are not formal around me, you won't be formal around anyone. Call them the Temples, or don't call them anything at all."

That ended the conversation for the evening.

20

I Don't Mind Taking Tea

The November day was frigid, and Samantha and William had already gone through several logs on the fire. They were both working in the sitting room, as it was the warmest room in the house, and Samantha almost rang for tea early, desiring to hold something warm in her hands.

The doorbell rang, and Mrs. Bishop attended to it.

Samantha looked up from her letters, expecting to see a sister, as no one else would come calling on such a day.

Elizabeth entered, still wearing her scarf, and went immediately to the fireplace to warm her hands. Her cheeks were rosy from the cold and her eyes were bright from her new romance.

"Aren't you freezing?" said Samantha.

"What? Oh yes, quite cold isn't it?" Elizabeth glanced about the room.

After a short moment to allow time for Elizabeth to state the purpose of her visit, William asked, "How did you find the grocers today?" He kept his eyes intently focused on the papers before him.

"I didn't go to the grocers yet," said Elizabeth.

"Well I'm very glad to know we haven't been forgotten." Samantha shoved her letters aside and made room for Elizabeth to sit. "Mrs. Bishop?" she called. "Will you bring tea?"

"Bring four cups, Mrs. Bishop," said Elizabeth. "Mr. Cole is on his way."

Samantha glanced sharply at William, who shook his head slightly to communicate that they must remain very calm and not do anything that might spook Elizabeth or Mr. Cole, even though they were both aware there was only one reason Elizabeth and Mr. Cole would turn up on the same day unexpectedly.

The doorbell rang again and William jumped up to answer it.

Samantha was exerting every fiber of energy into keeping her face neutral.

Mr. Cole's hair was disheveled, and he rubbed his hands as he joined Elizabeth by the fireplace. "Sorry I'm late. Alma Burros came by just as I was leaving. If I'd rushed out too quickly—you know."

"Of course, dear. I'm glad we decided to come separately. If she'd seen us together—"

"You're engaged!" Samantha leapt up, disrupting the neat pile of letters she'd just organized. She rushed to her sister, who was laughing and rolling her eyes at the same time.

William waited for a confirming nod from the beaming Mr. Cole before extending a hand of congratulations.

"This is splendid!" Samantha pulled Elizabeth down next to her. "What a wonderful surprise. But so soon? Did you not plan to wait?"

"We had planned to wait, yes. But then I suggested it might be a great comfort to Mrs. Cole to know her son would be well situated before Christmas, and Edward agreed."

"When did you propose?" Samantha glanced at Edward.

"Last evening. I had supper with your family and afterward Elizabeth and I visited the hothouse—it was too cold for anyplace else."

"Do the girls know?"

Elizabeth nodded. "I so wish we could have all been together, but Allison and Rose had their noses pressed against the kitchen window the whole time. They practically ambushed us when we came through the door. It was a dreadful sight."

Edward chuckled. "I'd never seen either of them so animated."

Mrs. Bishop entered with the tea. She beamed at Edward and Elizabeth and offered her own congratulations before retreating.

The brothers and sisters enjoyed a joyful hour of tea and celebration. Then Edward needed to return to the store and Elizabeth departed with him.

Samantha flung herself into William's arms the moment they were gone. "I don't even care about the challenge anymore. I'm just so happy. Did you see Edward's face? He looks positively ten years younger."

"Indeed," said William. "Honestly, I didn't agree with Allison and Rose's desire to throw them together.

Glad to know I was wrong. They're a perfect match, and now I'm wondering why I didn't see it before."

Samantha sank into the couch. "If we decide to make a living out of matchmaking, I'd say we'll need to enlist my sisters as foot soldiers."

William laughed. "I'll be happy when the year is done. We won't have to think about it anymore."

"But it has been rather fun, hasn't it?"

"At times, yes. Mostly, I've enjoyed working together with you."

"We make a good team, do we not?"

"A very good team."

"Now, we have about six weeks until the end of the year. What's our plan for Victoria?"

William laughed again. "Let us enjoy this moment of glory. Besides, if this is the end of our matches, I'd say we've done very well."

"I would really love to know Victoria is settled before we move to the coast."

"We shouldn't pack her off too quickly. If not for the challenge I'd say we leave her alone, let her enjoy her life as it is. Marriage will come soon enough, if it's to come at all."

Samantha reached a hand out to William and pulled him onto the couch beside her. "Do you want to know one of the reasons I fell in love with you?"

"I'm dashingly handsome and uproariously witty."

"You cared for my sisters so well. You understood my love for them. You even took this house so I could be near them, though I know it's been an inconvenience for your work at times."

"The trips have been a challenge, I won't lie. But I'd

do it all again. I adore your sisters, but most of all, I adore you. They make you happy, and I'll do anything to make you happy."

Samantha leaned her forehead against William's. "*You* make me happy," she whispered.

Friday afternoon was terribly frigid, but Victoria came just the same. They met in the conservatory, where Daniel had instructed her to come in the back way (to vex his mother, but he didn't tell Victoria this). When she entered, Daniel was sitting on a stone bench waiting.

"We'll explore the rest of the house today?" Victoria unwrapped herself from her shawl and sat down next to him.

"Brace yourself, Victoria," Daniel said.

"For what?"

"My mother is going to send you an invitation to take tea with her."

"Really? An invitation just for me?" Victoria's eyes lit up.

"Yes. If I know my mother it will be formal, complete with an R.S.V.P. Agnes Copeland."

"How exciting!"

"Yes."

"Why do you say it like that?"

"Like what?"

"Like you're annoyed."

"I'm not annoyed."

"Yes you are. It's only your mother."

"Exactly."

"Then why does it bother you so much? Do you not like taking tea?"

"I do not mind taking tea. When I'm in certain company."

"Oh, I see."

"My mother isn't exactly entertaining."

"Well neither are you."

Daniel was caught off guard and instantly sobered. He grunted, "I suppose I'm not."

Victoria nudged him. "I'm only joking. You are wonderful company. If you weren't, I wouldn't be coming here every day." She tilted her head, attempting to catch his eye.

Daniel forced a smile just for her.

"What will you be doing while we're having tea? Or are you going to join us?" Victoria asked.

"I'm scheduled to have tea with William and Samantha." Daniel held up his hands. "Forgive me, the Temples. My mother told me to call them the Temples."

Victoria giggled.

Daniel stood. "What are we waiting for? Let's look at the rest of the house. Do you want to start in the servants' quarters or in the cellar?"

Victoria opted for the cellar and soon discovered what she called a cellar and what the Copelands called a cellar were completely different things. The Copland's cellar was really another floor under ground. It had rooms for storage, though most of them were empty. The kitchen was situated at the far end of the cellar where several house staff were lounging lazily around the kitchen table.

Victoria wondered again what the Copelands needed so many servants for, but she decided not to ask.

They completed the cellar tour in less than half an hour, and Victoria sighed with relief when they reached the ground floor.

"Not much light or air down there, is there?" said Daniel.

"I suppose not."

"Now the attic?"

She nodded, and they went up the main staircase that ascended from the center of the atrium. At the end of the hall on the second floor was a door that led to the servants' staircase. Victoria remarked as they went up the narrow steps, "I bet your home is beautiful at Christmas."

"Not much different," said Daniel. "My mother orders a tree, and a wreath for the front door. That is all."

"Do you ever have parties?"

"No, not that I can recall."

"No parties? There is so much room. You could probably fit all of Tree Town just in the drawing room."

"No. It's just me and my mother most of the time."

"Then, forgive me for asking, what do you need all this space for?"

"Don't ask me. Ask my mother. After all, my father built it for her."

"What did she want it for?"

"Likely to show off how much money we had. She is very proud to be descended from an earl. I think there might have been many visitors, but that was all before my father died."

"Oh, I see. I am very sorry."

"There's nothing to be sorry about. I barely remember him."

"What did you do? I mean, when you were growing up?"

Daniel thought a moment as they reached the third floor. "I had a tutor. And I went to university for a year or so. I didn't like it, so I came home."

"Who were your friends? Who did you play with as a child?"

"You probably don't remember, but I used to play with your sisters."

"Did you? I don't remember that at all."

"It was a long time ago." Daniel noted that four years' difference in age (the difference between himself and Victoria) was not much when you were grown, but was quite a lot when you were children.

"Why did you stop?" Victoria asked.

"I suppose I just became bored. They were all such good friends, and preferred Ethan's company to mine. I chose to be alone."

"That's very sad."

"Why is it sad? It didn't bother me." Daniel led the way down the corridor. At the end of the hall he opened the door to the attic and was greeted by thick darkness. "I'm sorry. I should have thought to bring candles. Would you like to get some?"

"Let's save the attic for another day," said Victoria. "Want to go back to the conservatory? I like it in there."

They trekked back down the way they'd come, not saying much. When they reached the ground floor once again, Victoria spotted the piano. "Let's play," she said.

Daniel followed her to the instrument, and they squeezed next to one another on the bench. Instead of playing any songs they knew, they banged around on the keys, having a good laugh as they made up melodies, Daniel playing the right hand and Victoria playing the left.

Mrs. Copeland called from her parlor, "Stop that racket. If you're not going to play real music, don't play at all."

Victoria and Daniel smothered their laughter. Daniel began sorting through some sheet music to find a duet.

"Were you telling the truth back there, when you said it didn't bother you?" Victoria asked.

"What didn't bother me?"

"That my sisters were all good friends and they left you out."

Daniel's stomach dropped. He swung his legs around to the other side of the piano bench, shrugging. "I suppose it might have at first. I just got used to it."

"That was wrong of them to exclude you like that."

Daniel smiled. "It's over now. I don't think about it."

"But they still do it, don't they?"

Daniel stood up. "It's all right. Really. I don't mind." Daniel tried to think of a way to change the subject. His wit failed him (it was doing that quite often when he was with Victoria). Abruptly, he headed back to the conservatory.

Victoria followed behind him and went directly to a bench. Daniel took a seat opposite her.

"I feel left out sometimes too," she said softly.

Daniel's eyebrows lifted, surprised she wasn't letting the subject drop.

"That's why I like coming here. It's just you and me. I don't have to be anybody. You pay attention and you don't talk over me. Thank you for being kind to me, even though I'm a Hartford."

Daniel's eyebrows lifted further. A warm glow appeared at the base of his chest. It was an unfamiliar feeling. The warmth began to spread to the rest of his body as he surveyed the petite young women, with wild hair and piercing green eyes, sitting across from him.

Just then she was looking at him like he was genuinely her friend—had they really become friends in such a short time?

How else did she find it so easy to be open and honest?

"What are you doing?" Victoria asked.

"What do you mean?" Daniel stammered.

"Why are you looking at me like that?"

"Like what?"

"Like you want to say something but you're afraid."

Daniel nearly rolled his eyes. How did she do that? Marveling at how easily she could read him, he cleared his throat. "The truth is, I think your sisters have a good reason for not wanting to be near me. I ridicule and scold them to my heart's content, and it's got to be a real irritation sometimes. I don't blame them for wanting to keep their distance."

"Yes, I've heard them say something like that before."

Daniel felt that uncomfortable feeling in his stomach, the same one he'd felt when he and Samantha had argued. "I suppose, then, like most things, it's my fault."

Victoria stood up and crossed to sit beside him. "Well, I like you. And whatever it is that makes my sisters not like you, I'm sure it's a misunderstanding."

Daniel shrugged, then thought better of trying to divert the conversation and decided to give honesty a try. "I think that might be the first time anyone has said they liked me."

Instead of laughing, like he expected, Victoria tilted her head and analyzed him with her penetrating green eyes. "I wish we had been a bit closer in age," she finally said. "We could have been friends for each other when we were growing up. Sounds like we were both lonely children."

Surprised by this revelation as he was, Daniel couldn't help but think she'd given him new fodder for ridiculing the Hartfords. Not only would he be triumphant at the end of this year, but the perfectly amiable Hartford sisters were not so amiable— something he'd always suspected.

He smiled cheerfully. "It'll be getting dark soon. And it's dreadfully cold. I'll call a carriage to take you home."

"You don't have to do that."

"I couldn't very well let you walk home in this weather. Besides, my mother would be very disappointed if I did."

Victoria grinned. "Well, we mustn't disappoint your mother."

21

Don't Speak So Loudly Before Noon

At Sunday service, the town was abuzz with the news of Elizabeth Hartford and Edward Cole. The reverend very much wished he'd chosen a less weighty subject than the Second Coming, as not a soul in his parish paid any attention to a word he said. They were too busy glancing at the Hartfords and then swinging their heads toward the Cole family pew.

Afterwards, the new couple was swarmed with congratulations.

Only one person did not join in the celebration, standing glumly at the far end of the town hall, simmering in his ill-luck. Daniel was unprepared when Allison Hartford approached him, her arms crossed like she was holding herself back. "I've got some things to say to you," she said.

Behind Allison, Rose wrung her hands nervously. Not far off, Ethan was watching with an amused look on his face. Earlier, Rose had tried to convince him to curtail Allison's intention, but he'd refused. (Secretly he hoped the altercation would result in a bloody nose for Daniel.)

"What is the meaning of all this time you are spending with our sister?" Allison demanded.

Momentarily, Daniel blanched. His foot (which had been supporting him against the edifice) slipped down and he stood up straighter to keep from being pressed against the wall.

"Er...Beg pardon?" he said.

"You heard me. Everyone knows your opinion of the Hartford family. So I find it curious you're suddenly so friendly with one of us. Tell me at once, what are your intentions?"

Daniel rooted around his brain for a plausible explanation. Without revealing the challenge, his time with Victoria seemed—unusual—considering his typical disdain for the Hartfords.

If it hadn't been for the challenge, he'd never have attempted to become friends with Victoria and Elizabeth. What reason could he possibly give to the sister who now stood before him, balling her fists and preparing to pummel him if he made a misstep?

"We're only riding. I have a horse that needs exercise and Victoria wanted to learn." He shrugged lazily.

"But you haven't been riding, have you? It's been too cold or too rainy. You spend nearly all day together and I want to be sure you're not planning to break her heart."

At this, Daniel grinned. Then he laughed directly in Allison's face. "Dear Lord, Allison, with all these engagements in your family, afraid I might want a piece of the pie?" He laughed harder and Allison's face changed from anger-red to embarrassed-red.

Rose drew closer and took hold of Allison's arm. "We just want to make sure you are being careful, that is all."

"Careful about what?" Daniel expostulated. "You're insane if you think I'd ever fall for a Hartford."

"We just want to make sure you aren't taking advantage of our little sister. She's not like the rest of us. She's sensitive, and if you were to abuse her trust—just promise you'll take care?"

Daniel continued grinning. "Of course I will. What sort of monster do you take me for?"

Allison recovered, and she took a step closer. "Hurt her, and you'll answer to me."

Daniel rolled his eyes with exaggeration. "Go on, Allison, don't you have a wedding to plan?" He brushed past her and tipped his hat menacingly at Ethan. New Year's Day—the day of his triumph—couldn't come fast enough.

He marched home, smarting from the disappointment of Elizabeth's engagement and Allison and Rose's suggestion he might have ill-motives for his friendship with Victoria.

As if he could hurt Victoria if he wanted to. Like her, when they were together, he forgot he was Daniel Copeland, a man with a vendetta against the world and one family in particular.

She brought a cheerfulness to his day and there was no question he enjoyed her company.

Perhaps he was in danger of falling in love with her after all.

He laughed at the absurdity of such a notion.

Just before he reached home, an idea burst into his imagination, one he felt would delight Victoria, and he could not wait to tell her when she came on Monday. He whistled as he tramped up the steps, through the doorway, and into his mother's sitting room (she had already arrived home, as she always took the carriage and chided Daniel every week for walking to and fro like a pauper).

"Mother! I think we should have a dinner party."

"Daniel, don't speak so loudly before noon."

"What do you think?"

"Of what?"

"My idea to have a dinner party?"

"What is this you are saying? Explain yourself."

"We have a large house, and we don't use half of it. Why not share the blessings that God has bestowed upon us by having a dinner party here this Christmas?" Daniel began to pace, using his hands as he spoke. "We could hire a small orchestra, get the tree a little early, but instead of putting it in the foyer, let us put it in the drawing room. We could open all the doors and windows to air it out and then use that room as a dance floor. It's large enough. We could invite everyone in town. I'm sure they would come. There hasn't been an event like this for as long as I can remember." He placed his hands behind his back and turned to face his mother. "Well?"

Though Mrs. Copeland had never in her life seen her son so animated, the thought of having so many people in her home disturbed her. True, she'd had many parties before her husband had passed on (God rest him). But that was years ago. Dancing and eating till all hours? Opening the windows in the middle of winter?

Such a thought was just short of terrifying.

She watched his face fall when she began to shake her head. "No Daniel. I don't want strangers in our home. Besides, it would be such an expense."

Daniel's usual slouching posture returned, but instead of beginning an argument (as Agnes Copeland expected), he merely shrugged. "Thank you for thinking over my request." He clicked his heels together like a soldier and turned to go, stopping at the door to say, "Good morning, Mother" before departing.

Daniel went on a long walk to brood. Thoughts of self-pity consumed him as he used a stick to whack at the brambles that impeded his path.

He was still brooding the next day when Victoria arrived at the stables. "It's been a long time since we've ridden," she said. "I've missed it."

Daniel didn't say a word as he mounted and waited for Victoria to climb on to Angel. They were off, but not very happily.

"What is bothering you?" asked Victoria.

"Just another disappointed idea, that's all."

"What was the idea?"

"I wanted to throw a dinner party at Christmas, but my mother detested the thought."

"You wanted to have a dinner party? How marvelous! Why did she say no?"

"Because she's bitter, cynical, selfish, and self-absorbed, that's why."

"That is not at all true. Well, not all of it, anyway."

"You would say that. You've only spent one day with her."

Victoria reigned her horse to a stop. Daniel stopped to look back at her, feeling a pang of guilt. "I'm sorry," he said. "I didn't mean to take it out on you. It's not your fault."

"That's not it. But you are upset. I am sorry your scheme was thwarted. It was a lovely idea. But I know your mother loves you and is proud of you. She just doesn't know what to do with you."

"Did she tell you that?"

"No, but it wasn't difficult to see. She doesn't seem the sort to admit her feelings of regard. In that way, her son is very like her."

"I truly hope not."

They began to ride again, and for the first time he wondered if he didn't try to understand his mother any more than she tried to understand him.

22

She Prefers Not to Fraternize With Commoners

Daniel was quiet during tea. Samantha had decided not to broach the subject of Elizabeth's engagement, half expecting Daniel to bring it up anyway. But he didn't. Rather than his usual barbs of sarcasm, he seemed deep in thought (a side of him, Samantha admitted, she had never seen before).

"Victoria is having tea with your mother today?" she asked.

"Yes." Daniel reached out to accept the offered cup of tea.

"She told me she was looking forward to it. She really likes your mother."

Daniel grunted.

"Hard for you to believe?"

"Not really. Victoria seems to like everybody."

"Yes, she's always had a gift for finding the good in people."

"A skill I've always lacked." Daniel stared at his tea, lost in thought again.

Samantha watched him with amusement.

William entered just then, looking a bit disheveled and slightly bleary-eyed. He poured himself tea, and Daniel noted that William always poured himself tea. Considering it was typically the role of the servant or the lady of the house, for the first time since forming an acquaintance with Samantha's husband, he understood why the eldest Hartford sister had become attached to him.

He certainly wasn't like other men.

As William sat next to Samantha, she said, "I don't think I've ever really gotten to know your mother."

"She prefers not to fraternize with commoners." Daniel gave himself a high, nasally sounding voice, and exaggerated the extension of his pinky to emphasize her snobbery.

Samantha smiled. "How on earth did little Victoria slide into her good graces?"

Daniel shrugged.

"It's widely known she is the granddaughter of an Earl." Samantha stated for William's benefit.

"She will be delighted to hear it's widely known, considering it's her greatest joy in life," Daniel said.

"She must find our little town very lonely."

"She's always been contented to be alone."

"I'm sure you are a great comfort to her."

At this, Daniel chuckled. "More like a thorn responsible for her gray hair. At least that's what she tells me."

Samantha and William laughed. "I suppose family

has a way of irking us in a way no one else can," William said.

"But not so for the Hartfords." Daniel raised his cup in salute.

"You'd be surprised..." Samantha trailed off.

"What's this? Are you suggesting the nigh-perfect Hartfords are not always walking in familial harmony?"

"There he is. I was worried the real Daniel might have gotten lost somewhere." Samantha smiled at him.

Daniel grinned back.

"So, how are the riding lessons coming along?" William asked.

"Just fine," Daniel responded, but decided he no longer wished to speak about Victoria to her relations. "And the move to the coast? Is there a date set?"

Taking the diversion in stride, William responded, "We'll likely secure a house the next time we return. After Christmas."

"Such a long sojourn in Tree Town."

"Business will slow closer to the holidays."

"A much needed slowing down," Samantha added.

"But you will be here for New Year's?" Daniel asked slyly.

Both Samantha and William looked at Daniel squarely. He crossed one leg over the other, and smiled. "I'd hate for you to miss the opportunity to admit your defeat."

"Darling," said Samantha to William. "I think Mr. Copeland might not have heard the news about Elizabeth and Edward."

"No one could escape the knowledge," said Daniel. "I think the town might be getting suspicious."

"It's true," said William. "Dr. Vaughn asked if there was some sort of magic potion being used. Odd question from a man of science."

"I'll admit I never thought we'd get this far," said Samantha.

"You've done very well indeed," Daniel said gallantly. "But assure me you'll not be disappearing before New Year's?"

"Are you not crowing a bit too loudly, too early?

"Of course not. Victoria is securely in my trap and not likely to leave now that she's befriended my mother."

"I do hope you have a plan for explaining all of this to her. Remember your promise?"

"Of course I remember. She'll not be injured."

Samantha sighed. "Laying the challenge aside, what do you think of Elizabeth and Mr. Cole?"

"Not a match I would have ever expected."

"We're quite surprised ourselves."

"They seem...happy."

"They do. Which is everything I could have hoped for."

Daniel chewed the inside of his mouth and began to contemplate a folly in the challenge. The whole scheme had succeeded in securing an increase of happiness for a family that was already entirely too happy.

He glanced at the clock on the mantel and thought he might leave a little early, so as not to miss seeing Victoria before she left his mother.

For two full weeks, Victoria and Daniel rode every day, but on a Friday afternoon, Victoria requested to explore the attic. She was beginning to come down with a cold, and her mother threatened to keep her home entirely if she did not stay indoors.

They were passing through the front foyer when they saw Mrs. Copeland, separated from her usual post, and standing by a table with a short, wiry man in a dark suit. The table was covered with pieces of paper, and the man was peering through his spectacles as he showed two distinct documents to Daniel's mother.

Mrs. Copeland looked up as they entered and immediately came around the table with an unusual spring of energy. "Victoria, come here. I'd like your opinion on something."

Victoria went to her and was shown the two pieces of paper by the little gentleman.

"Which do you think would be best," asked Mrs. Copeland. "Silver or gold embossing?"

Victoria took both sheets of paper in her hands. Daniel slid to stand just behind her, curiosity stirring. He read: *You are cordially invited by the household of Copeland to attend a dinner party on the 20th of December, 5 o'clock in the evening at the Copeland Estate in Whinn County R.S.V.P. A. Copeland*

Daniel's eyes grew large, and he had to clench his teeth to keep his jaw from dropping. He floundered to regain his composure when he realized his mother was watching him out of the corner of her eye.

"I like the silver," said Victoria. "It reminds me of a postcard that I saw once of snowflakes. Wouldn't it be wonderful if it snowed for your party?"

"No, dear, I don't think it would be wonderful," said Mrs. Copeland, as she snatched the papers back. "I think it would be dreadful. No one would come, and if they did, they would all catch cold."

"Will my family be receiving an invitation? I haven't been to this sort of dinner party in a very long time. And never in Tree Town."

"It is rude to request an invitation," said Mrs. Copeland. But Victoria only smiled in response. "Yes, your family will be invited. I expect you to show me your dress. You will have a new dress, won't you?"

"I'll ask Papa, but I'm sure he will say yes for this very special occasion."

"Now I don't want any fuss about it." Mrs. Copeland stared hard at Daniel. "Go back to what you were doing. I'm very busy here." Mrs. Copeland brushed them aside with a wave of her hand.

Daniel nodded, knowing this would be the last time they discussed it.

Victoria took Daniel's arm and steered him toward the conservatory. Once safely out of earshot, Victoria began to laugh. "You thought your mother was a hard-crusted, bitter old woman. But it seems she wants to have a jolly time just like the rest of us. I knew she cared more for you than you thought. She's doing this all for you, Daniel. You ought to be ashamed of yourself." She poked him in the arm and then stepped in front of him.

"You are wrong. She's doing this for you, but I find I'm not at all jealous."

Victoria laughed again. "We should practice dancing. It's been at least a year since I've attended a ball." She lifted her hands and beckoned Daniel closer.

Daniel coughed. "Right now?"

Victoria nodded.

"You'll find me a clumsy dance partner." Daniel took her firmly in his arms. An action that, for some reason, signaled his heart to start pounding before they even began to waltz.

Victoria was light and seemed to float as they whirled about the room, keeping perfect time to imaginary music. They moved as one unit and never took their eyes off one another.

Even as the pounding in his heart moved upwards to begin pounding in his ears, Daniel marveled at out perfectly they fit together.

They didn't miss a step.

When the song in their heads ended, they came to a stop directly in front of the fountain, both breathing heavily.

Victoria dropped her arms. "That was beautiful. You are a wonderful dancer. You will dance with me at the party, won't you? I know the man is supposed to ask, but we don't care about such formalities, do we?" She turned away and headed back into the house.

Daniel held his hand over his heart. It was hurting, but it wasn't from the dance. After a few steadying breaths, he followed after Victoria.

23

I've Tolerated You For Twenty-Two Years

"Someone knock me over with a feather," said Mr. Hartford, as he stared at a card in his hand over breakfast. He peered through his spectacles and then asked Mrs. Hartford to verify he was seeing things clearly. "Is this some sort of joke?" asked Mrs. Hartford, taking the card from her husband.

"What is it?" asked Elizabeth.

"An invitation to a Christmas party at the Copeland Estate."

"Are you serious?" exclaimed Allison, who bolted out of her chair and circled around behind her mother. Rose and Elizabeth joined her and they all stared dumbfounded at the invitation.

Victoria delicately spread butter on her scone. She glanced up when she realized her family was staring at her. "Yes," she responded to their silent inquisition. "It was all Daniel's idea, but his mother has put it in motion. You should see the house. It's going to be lovely. Might I have a new dress, Father?"

"May I have a new dress, too?" asked Rose.

"And I?" said Elizabeth and Allison.

Mr. Hartford was still pale with shock. "Of course. I think I shall have a new dress too."

The sisters gathered around Victoria and began peppering her with questions.

For a few days together, wedding plans were forgotten.

In anticipation of the upcoming dinner party, which was now only three weeks away, Mrs. Copeland suggested that Daniel and Victoria practice dancing together. They agreed to submit themselves to her tutelage, so Mrs. Copeland tuned her piano, stretched out her wrinkled fingers, and accompanied her young students while she shouted instructions to them from the bench.

"Daniel, we should be exceedingly proud of ourselves," said Victoria as they were dancing a slow waltz one afternoon.

"How so?" Daniel found he often became lost in Victoria's green eyes, which always seemed to be shimmering no matter what light they were in.

"Everything we do together we do well. Be it riding, dancing, exploring, or whatever else we set our minds to. We are an unstoppable pair, you and I."

"Now that you mention it," Daniel lifted his arm for Victoria to spin under. "I think you're right. For this reason I believe we should take careful consideration before we ever toy with the idea of separating."

"Have you ever thought about separating?"

"I have wondered if you would ever grow tired of coming here."

Victoria grew very serious. "Have you really?"

"Yes, you couldn't possibly want to keep coming here forever."

"Do you want me to stop coming?"

Daniel shook his head violently. "Absolutely not. I enjoy having you around." The dancing couple did not notice that their pace had increased and Mrs. Copeland began to play faster to keep up with them.

"Are you sure?" Victoria asked intently.

"Of course I'm sure. Have I ever indicated differently?"

"Would you tell me if you ever grew tired of me?"

Daniel chuckled. "I can't imagine ever growing tired of you."

"But what if you did?"

The music came to a stop, but Daniel clung firmly to Victoria so she would know he was serious. "It is more likely you would grow tired of me. Not many people can tolerate me for very long."

"I've tolerated you for twenty-two years," said Mrs. Copeland from the piano.

Daniel and Victoria both smiled and turned their heads in her direction. "Agree with me, Mother," said Daniel. "Victoria will never exhaust her welcome in the Copeland home, will she?"

"I agree wholeheartedly. She's quite become a member of the family." She shuffled through some sheet music as Daniel and Victoria set up for the next dance.

"How about that Irish jig you were teaching us yesterday?" he requested, feeling he desperately needed a dance that could keep pace with his racing heart.

Afterward, Daniel couldn't push the idea away that Victoria was becoming a permanent addition to the scenery of the estate. What would happen if she really did grow tired of coming every day? When this thought entered, he would shake his head and remind himself to enjoy the happiness she brought with her while it lasted.

Victoria was full of excitement over little things about which Daniel had never taken time to ponder. One of which was the litter of puppies that one of the last remaining foxhounds had birthed. Victoria cooed over them and begged Daniel to raise the puppies as hunters so she might learn to fox hunt. Daniel agreed, though he knew there was little chance she'd still be visiting once the puppies were old enough for the hunt.

He made the decision, with great force of will, should the interests of her young heart turn in a different direction—as they surely would someday— he must unselfishly let her go.

Someone else was noticing a difference that Victoria Hartford had unknowingly made in the Copeland home. Mrs. Copeland wisely kept quiet about the remarkable change in her brooding and selfish son. He laughed a little more and began to pay more attention when she spoke. He didn't come to supper with a grudge already formed and didn't roll his eyes when she requested he ride home with her from Sunday service. For this reason, Agnes Copeland encouraged him to spend as much time with Victoria as he could.

Three days before the Christmas party (an event that had caused a great stir among the Tree Town residents and had momentarily taken all attention off the prospect of Hartford weddings) Daniel was brimming with excitement when he entered the stables. "I've got a surprise for you," he said as soon as he saw Victoria. He playfully brushed a finger on her chin on his way to tend to his horse.

"What is it?" Victoria asked.

"Mother and I want you to be queen of the party."

"Really?" she exclaimed. She ran to him and threw her arms around his neck. "I'd love to!"

Daniel took her hands and gazed at her. He could imagine her, standing by his side as the guests thronged into the foyer. She was smiling, nodding, and kissing cheeks. Just as a real queen would.

"What would I have to do?" she asked, removing her hands from his and returning to her duties with Angel.

"Nothing. Just smile and greet people as they come in the door."

"Sounds like a lot of work," she said playfully.

"It will be easy for you. Mother and I think it'd be best. I'm not good with large crowds of people and Mother gets tired easily. We'll need your energy at the party. You'll make a marvelous hostess and they'll call you the belle of the ball."

Victoria curtsied dramatically. "Why thank you, kind sir."

"My pleasure, milady." Daniel bowed.

They smiled at each other and turned back to their horses. Daniel shook his head, as he'd just worked out a mystery, the reason behind his lost appetite, little sleep (though he was never tired), and the constant sensation in his heart that he hadn't been able to account for.

Furthermore, he found himself in a remarkably good humor whenever he was in Victoria's presence—just thinking of her (which he was prone to do regularly) was enough to raise his spirits. He shook his head again as he mounted Ebony.

He'd never been in love, but he was not ignorant of its signs.

Things were not turning out the way he had planned.

"Mother is not feeling well today," Daniel told Victoria when she arrived the next day. He was waiting for her on the front steps, looking very small sitting on the grand stone stairs.

Victoria walked up beside him and sat down. "Shall we ride, or shall we practice dancing on our own?"

"What would you like to do?" Unconsciously, he moved so his knees were resting against hers.

"Let's practice dancing in the conservatory. It's my favorite spot in your house. And in there we won't disturb your mother."

Daniel rose to his feet and gave Victoria his hand, but he did not relinquish it after helping her up. To his pleasure, she didn't pull away.

"The dinner party is the day after tomorrow, and I can hardly wait," Victoria said, as they strolled down the path leading around the side of the house to the conservatory.

"Yes, hard to believe. Never in a million years did I think I'd see the day."

"Wait till everyone sees you dance. They'll be astonished."

"Wait till every sees *you* dance. They'll be ashamed to share the same dance floor."

"I don't think so. My sisters are very good dancers. I saw Ethan and Allison practicing on the hill. They dance very well."

They fell silent as they neared the back of the house.

Before going inside Victoria asked, "Who else are you going to dance with?"

"What do you mean?" Daniel glanced down at her.

"You can't dance with me the whole time, you know?"

"I can't?"

Victoria laughed. "Of course not. It'd cause a scene."

"I don't care."

Victoria laughed again, but stopped abruptly when she realized Daniel wasn't joining her. She tugged on his hand and turned him to face her.

He felt the sudden urge to run, but Victoria's hand, and his own desire, kept him rooted where he stood.

An unseen fog settled upon them, and his thoughts—his reasoning—disappeared. He couldn't remember the last time he had thought rationally concerning the angel standing in front of him. He had no concept of the time they stood, under the shadow of the big Copeland house, gazing at one another. As in a dream, he pulled her closer to himself.

And kissed her.

The moment his lips met hers, time seemed to stop. The softness, the tenderness of her mouth sent pleasure surging through his core—a feeling like nothing he'd ever experienced.

Then, by some miracle of heaven, Victoria was leaning into his kiss. The hand that had been gripping his slid free and ran up his arm to his shoulder, leaving a tingling sensation in every place it touched.

It was magic. Daniel wanted her closer. He wrapped his arms around her, and for just one moment, it was perfect.

Until Victoria gasped and turned her face away. When he pulled back and looked into her eyes, there were tears. Her sad smile, the step backwards, and then the slow shaking of her head, cut through his heart, replacing the warmth of the kiss with an ice-cold shame.

He turned and walked away. The walking quickly became a run.

24

The Cad Had Us Jinxed

Victoria stumbled home in a daze of stunned silence. The moment she entered the house, her body quivered with a great sob, and she quickly ran upstairs and closed herself in her room.

It wasn't long before one of her sisters deduced something was wrong and sought to discover the reason for Victoria's distress. However, Victoria barred Rose from entrance, though Rose could hear her sniffling on the other side.

Next, Allison, then Elizabeth tried their hand at coaxing, but still Victoria refused to see them. Knowing she had just returned from the Copeland Estate, their alarm was growing by the minute, so they dispatched Allison to town.

Allison did not wait for Mrs. Bishop to announce her to Samantha. Bursting through the door, she declared, "Victoria's been in her room crying ever since she returned from the Copelands."

This was all the information Samantha needed to

don her winter attire and venture into the descending night as Allison led the way.

Once arriving at the Hartfords, Samantha went directly to Victoria's room, where Rose and Elizabeth were keeping watch. They crowded round the door as Samantha prepared to knock, but before she did, she said, "No, no, you must wait downstairs. Elizabeth, I'm counting on you to keep them there." She shooed them away amidst their looks of protest, then rapped softly on the door. "Tori? It's Samantha."

The door flew open, revealing a disheveled and red-nosed Victoria. "Samantha! Whatever are you doing here?"

Samantha shrugged. "They called in the cavalry."

Victoria glanced about to be sure it was safe, then she pulled Samantha into her room. Immediately she broke down crying into her older sister's arms until Samantha finally asked, "Darling, what's this all about?"

Victoria pulled away. "Stupid, stupid, stupid. Of all the stupid things. This had to happen now? Why couldn't it have waited just a few more days? Now everything is ruined and there's nothing to be done."

Samantha sank onto Victoria's bed. "Victoria, did something happen between you and Daniel?"

"Yes!" Victoria cried. "I'm angry and feel stupid and wish it would all go away."

"What would go away?"

Victoria seemed not to hear her. "If it could have just waited a few more days. The party is the day after tomorrow. I was supposed to be queen. Daniel and I were to lead the dances. Now it's all ruined."

"Is that what's upsetting you?"

"Of course it is! I've been looking forward to this. All of you have weddings and marriages and moves to the coast. This was mine. My happy moment for which we've been practicing and dancing and decorating. The house is so beautiful. And I was to sit at the head of the table and now all of that is ruined."

The picture of what was troubling Victoria slowly began to form in Samantha's mind. A smidge of anger simmered in her belly as she realized her caution to Daniel had gone unheeded. Though this wasn't what she'd been afraid of—in fact she was just a little surprised. "What exactly did Daniel do?" she asked.

Victoria glanced at her, as if it were obvious.

"Oh," Samantha said, eyes growing big.

"You mustn't blame him," said Victoria. "I told you because I know you are friends. The others will not understand. They already hate him. I'm sure he is very angry with himself. You'll go to him, won't you? Make sure he's all right?"

"My duty is to you. And I'm not leaving until I am assured *you* are all right."

Victoria began crying again. "I don't know what I feel, but foremost in my mind is that my family will have reason to dislike Daniel forever. Please don't tell anyone? If it can be kept a secret and then forgotten I believe I might feel better."

"He is a grown man and must bear the consequences for what he's done."

"And everything will be different now when it was so perfect before."

"Yes, it cannot be the same. You mustn't go there anymore."

"There is no danger of that. I suppose that means I can't attend the party. I've been fighting a cold anyways, so I believe I should stay back."

"If you don't go, our family will know something is wrong."

"You're right. Nobody knew I was supposed to be queen. I'll just arrive and behave as any other guest would. But promise me you will speak to Daniel?"

"It is too late this evening. But I will go tomorrow."

"Thank you. Oh, thank you. I don't know what I'd do without you."

Samantha remained calm and empathetic as Victoria cried some more. Then Victoria said she was tired and went to bed directly.

On her way back into town, however, Samantha seethed with rage at Daniel for breaking his promise. Then she mourned for her sister, who had lost her companion. Then she was disappointed in Victoria for encouraging such behavior. Then she blamed herself for naively believing Daniel's general dislike of the Hartfords was enough to keep him from forming any attachment to one of the sisters. How could she have been so foolish as to think so much time alone would be appropriate for any young man and woman without some sort of understanding? So ardently had her parents fought to create a world of freedom and safety for their daughters, perhaps they had forgotten to teach Victoria of the real world in which a woman's reputation could be ruined very easily while the man might (and often did) escape unscathed.

Then it was time to blame her parents for not keeping a closer eye on their youngest daughter and neglecting to teach her propriety.

And then, what had Mrs. Copeland been thinking? She was commonly known for her devotion to custom and could not have been ignorant of how much time Victoria spent with her son.

Or perhaps she was very aware and hoped a match might be made.

This thought caused Samantha to fume with rage again, as she felt her sister had been sorely used by the whole Copeland family.

Then there was the matter of Victoria feeling neglected by her sisters as they planned for their upcoming weddings. The poor girl had practically been driven into Daniel's arms by loneliness, and this all circled back around to Samantha once again blaming herself.

After all, she had the knowledge of the situation and might have prevented it. She was not without influence over Daniel (however stubborn and roguish he appeared to be) and she felt sure he would have listened to her had she asked him to take certain precautions for her sister's protection.

By the time Samantha reached home, she concluded that it was all her fault. Victoria was lively and pretty. It made perfect sense bored, purposeless Daniel would become attached. That the kiss had happened was dreadfully unfortunate, but her resolve to be fair when she sought him out was firmly in place by the time she relayed the events of the day to her husband.

William proceeded through the same cycle of rage as Samantha, muttering, "What was he thinking?"

over and over as Samantha sent for tea and waited for him to stop pacing.

It was a good hour before he calmed down. Samantha made him promise before she told him anything that he would not take action, no matter how badly he wished to go to the Copeland estate and avenge Victoria. He'd obliged, but it was very difficult. Finally, he sank onto the sofa and accepted a prepared cup of tea.

"In the end it really is all our fault," said William. "If it hadn't been for the stupid challenge, this would have never happened."

"That is just my feeling," said Samantha. "Daniel should have been far more guarded, but from what Victoria told me, he was just as surprised by the kiss as she was."

"Poor Victoria. We should have sought out a match for her straight away. Why did we tarry? We had over a month left. We could have found some young man to agree to marry her."

"We did try, if you will recall. We offered to take her with us to the coast, but she told us she was too busy and the weather was too cold and she'd much rather visit in the spring."

"She was too busy spending time with Daniel. The cad had us jinxed and we didn't even know it. And now we are suffering the consequences—or rather *she* is suffering the consequences. Ought your parents to be told?"

"Only if Victoria wishes to. They will be very disappointed I'm sure, but she is of age and her choices are hers. If she does choose to tell them, I know they will put the blame in the proper place."

"Not on us, as they are ignorant of our involvement."

"Only until New Year's, remember?"

"Right. Perhaps you could use this situation as leverage with Daniel to get us out of that."

"I'll do my best."

"No matter what happens tomorrow, remember Daniel did break his promise to us, and for that he does *not* deserve your pity."

"Don't worry, husband, Daniel will not escape without feeling the depth of his folly."

Daniel had gone out early in the morning to ride. He had barely slept during the night, so as soon as he saw the gray light of dawn, he threw himself out of bed and went to the stables.

He was gone all morning, only to return when he was quite exhausted, though his misery had not abated.

He nearly fell out of the saddle when Samantha stepped out from one of the stalls.

On instinct, he reached for his usual armor of cynicism and sarcasm. To his dismay, they would not respond to his call, and he was forced to ask in a raw, unguarded voice, "What are you doing here?"

"Hello, Daniel."

He shuddered when the greeting stirred the memory of a younger sister who used to greet him the same way.

"Might I impose on you for a walk? Your grounds are simply splendid."

Daniel made no response but headed out of the stables, Samantha close behind. He walked on for some time, knowing if he stopped, she'd start to speak, and he was sure he didn't want to hear what she had to say.

Finally, they reached a cove of wood where many stones lay strewn about, as if someone moved them there for a sort of town counsel. Daniel took a seat on one.

"I apologize for ambushing you," said Samantha. "I thought if I sent a note ahead, you might refuse to see me." She took a seat on the stone opposite his. "I came to see how you are, but it seems you are not well."

After a long silence, Daniel said, "How you must despise me."

Samantha straightened. "I cannot deny I am disappointed. But please know, I don't despise you."

"How could you not? I did the very thing I promised not to do—tamper with Victoria's heart."

There was a long—very uncomfortable—silence in which Samantha observed him. He felt himself shrinking under her gaze and prepared himself for the reprimand he knew he deserved.

Finally she spoke. "Daniel, I cannot fault you for falling in love with my sister. Yes, don't look so surprised. I've spent most of this year trying to bring people together and help them fall in love. I know what love looks like, and it's all over your face. It is because of your promise—and your vested interest in not becoming attached—that leads me to conclude your affection is genuine. How could I fault you for that?"

Daniel shifted, and he realized if there were anyone he wished to ask for counsel, she was sitting right in front of him. "I must confess I feel quite lost."

"I can imagine this was unexpected."

"You must believe me that I never once thought something like this would happen."

"Of course you didn't."

"Now I've gone and ruined everything—just like I always do. I wish I could take everything back. I wish I had more self-control—I wish—I wish this had never happened."

"But it did. Now the question is, what do you intend to do about it?"

"Tell me what to do, I'll do anything."

"No, this one's for you to solve. Though I'll certainly help. First, what's your plan for the Christmas ball?"

Daniel felt his face turn cold. "I'd forgotten all about it. I can't cancel, can I?"

"You could, but there'd be a lot of disappointed people."

"What would you do?"

"I cannot answer that. But I will say, if you choose to keep the date, William and I will attend, in all our splendor." She raised her hand dramatically.

"And the rest of your family?"

"I cannot speak for them. But as of today they are ignorant of what passed between you and my sister."

Daniel sat back. "She didn't tell them?"

"She only confided in me."

While this news came as a relief, it puzzled Daniel. He'd spent the night worrying over how he'd treated Victoria, but a small part of his misery was the knowledge he had sealed his fate in the eyes of the Hartfords. Until then, he had not realized how he'd come to value their opinion of him, and could only attribute it to his sudden, unexpected feelings for Victoria.

The thought of being in the same room as Victoria caused Daniel's chest to lose air. His heart pounded, and he felt hot and cold all at the same time.

But then again, she might not come.

But then again, every time Daniel thought Victoria wouldn't show, she always did. She wasn't a coward like he was. If the ball continued, she would attend.

He thought perhaps he should cancel, if only to give Victoria the excuse she needed to not see him.

Samantha waited while he waged his inner battle. With a large inhale of winter air, Daniel declared the ball would continue as planned, though he dreaded telling his mother Victoria would no longer be queen of the party.

"Will you do something for me?" he asked. "Will you deliver a note to Victoria?"

"What do you intend to say?"

"Just that I will understand completely if she wishes to stay away."

"Perhaps I'll tell her in person. A letter might cause alarm."

"Of course, I hadn't thought of that."

"It's going to be all right, Daniel." She smiled to put him at ease, but he felt anything but easy about the next few days.

After she left, his misery increased. She'd gone entirely too easy on him. He'd treated Victoria abominably, yet Samantha seemed bent on helping him. She even offered to dance the first two dances in Victoria's place.

As he poured his heart into the final preparations leading up to the Christmas ball, he counted the hours until the entire scheme would be behind him.

25

You Had So Many Friends

The evening of the Christmas dinner party, Daniel brooded in his room an hour before guests were scheduled to arrive. How had he managed to make such a mess of things? If he'd had more self-control, Victoria would be arriving to assist him with hosting, and they would be amiable and easy without a care in the world.

The joy of the preparations had dissipated by the time he informed his mother that Victoria would no longer be queen of the party. It had been the most difficult thing he had done that week. He would have preferred that she fly at him and call him all sorts of names. Instead she sat silent, with her lips pursed together. When he had finished telling her the whole story, she said, "Well, my boy, I guess it will just be you and me again."

The words cut him deeply. He left this audience with his mother feeling like he had disappointed her one final time. He'd cried hot, angry tears. Then he pulled himself together. He just needed to make it through the dinner party. He could wallow in self-pity once it was done.

Daniel stormed out of his room, putting his suit jacket on as he did so. At the top of the stairs he stopped suddenly. His mother was coming out of her room, wearing her gown. The usual black silk was gone. Now she wore a pale satin with delicate beadwork and chiffon overlay. It hugged her slim figure. The gray in her hair looked almost silver and was loosely pulled back with combs decorated to match her gown. She looked fifteen years younger. Only when she spoke was Daniel convinced it was still his mother.

"Don't gawk. I can still get dressed up. And don't act like I'm some phantom. I feel uncomfortable enough as it is."

Daniel snapped his mouth shut and offered her his arm with a smile. "You look lovely."

She surveyed him and reached up to straighten his collar before she took his arm. "You've cleaned up nicely. You actually look a lot like your father, God rest him."

They walked down the stairs together.

The foyer sparkled as it had never sparkled before. The candles in the windows gave it an ethereal but cozy atmosphere. Any minute, guests would be arriving.

One of those guests, Daniel was in dread of seeing. If she chose to attend.

At 5 o'clock, the first guests arrived. The stable hands became footmen and helped the guests out of their carriages. Tree Town turned out a completely different set of ladies and gentlemen. Daniel was impressed at how much time everyone seemed to have put into their dress for the occasion. Everyone was polished and shimmering and oozing with compliments for the Copeland home.

Daniel was distracted for a few minutes when the musicians sought his instruction for the dinner set and the selection for the first dance. He missed the entrance of the Hartfords, but he knew Victoria had come—as he had predicted she would.

He kept her in the corner of his eye as he greeted other guests. She was wearing pale blue. She always wore pale blue. It suited her. Obviously, Victoria was aware of that fact. She did not pay him any attention, and when she smiled and curtsied to greet his mother, he could tell her smile was forced.

When it was time for the first dance, Samantha appeared at his side. He'd never been more grateful in his life. She led the first two dances confidently, and the applause following each set assured Daniel his guests were pleased.

After a few more sets, Daniel found himself near Victoria. He turned to face her, though for her sake, he desperately wanted to be on the other side of the room. She smiled cordially. "Your home is beautiful," she said. "You and your mother outdid yourselves. Everything is wonderful."

"Thank you for coming," he said.

Victoria blushed and looked awkwardly away.

The music began, and Daniel inclined his head in the direction of the dance floor. "I hope—whatever has happened this past week, will be forgotten. Will you honor me with a dance?" He extended his hand with dread and watched her face closely.

She smiled and slowly placed her hand in his. Daniel let out his breath and led her to the dance floor.

"This is the waltz, you know." Daniel attempted the start of a casual conversation. But he only felt stupid.

"I didn't want to come tonight." Her eyes were downcast.

"I'm sorry." Daniel did not withhold his remorse as he concentrated intently on Victoria's every expression.

She shivered, nearly imperceptibly. "It was not for the reason you might think. I was afraid I might not remain composed, and my family will know something went wrong."

"It was kind of you, not to expose my behavior. Though you had every right."

"I'm not ashamed of you, if that is what you are thinking."

"Are you not?"

"No."

"Then you do know it is customary to look at your partner while you dance with him?"

Victoria raised her eyes to his for the remainder of the dance, but she didn't smile.

Daniel wished he hadn't said anything.

They stopped spinning as the waltz concluded, but they continued looking into each other eyes, asking a thousand silent questions. Daniel wasn't aware he was still holding on to her until a voice interrupted him.

"Daniel, would you dance with me?" It was Samantha.

"I'd like a dance with my little sister." That was William.

Daniel escaped into the next dance with Samantha, feeling hounded from every direction. He wanted to flee the party, but he mustn't.

Dance with Samantha. Smile. Forget that the party was for Victoria. It was now for the guests. He must think about the guests. He must think about his mother. Forget that he had disappointed the few people in his life who had believed in him. Start over. Earn back their trust.

As that dance concluded, he asked Elizabeth to be his partner for the next. She looked astonished, but then accepted kindly. When the dance finished, he asked Allison. Next was Rose. Finally, Mrs. Hartford. Then, for the last two dances before supper, he convinced his mother to dance with him. Though she complained about her aching feet, she smiled and even laughed when he spun her about the room.

There was more music during supper. Daniel didn't sit down. He went from table to table speaking amiably with everyone. Dr. and Mrs. Vaughn, Edward Cole, Loretta Humphrey, Alma Burros, Mr. and Mrs. Sommers, Ethan Clay, Reuben Dudley, the reverend, and countless others who had simply been faces with names though he had known them his entire life.

More dancing came after dessert. Daniel mingled with one crowd and then another. Laughing with them, hearing their stories, acquainting himself with a large part of Tree Town he had missed, due to his disinterest over the years.

One o'clock in the morning became two o'clock before the last guest departed. The air was cold and biting, but Daniel stood at the door and said good night to each person as they left. They showered him with compliments of which he felt undeserving.

When the front doors closed with a thud, the house was ominously silent.

Daniel leaned his forehead against the doors as weariness flooded his body. He felt heavy as he turned around.

He came face to face with his mother.

"I shall die from being up so late, but I rather enjoyed that." She grinned girlishly. "Thank you for making this happen. I couldn't have done it without you. You were charming." She reached out and patted his cheek tenderly.

Daniel managed a smile.

"What is wrong, my love?" The corners of her eyes wrinkled with concern.

"I'm just tired," he answered honestly.

"You ought to be. You have had a trying week. But you pulled through nicely. I had no idea you had so many friends in this town."

Friends. The word felt strange to his ears.

The butler appeared in the foyer. "The musicians have gone," he reported. "If you won't be needing me, Mr. Copeland, I shall retire for the evening."

"Absolutely, thank you Mr. Phillips." Daniel exerted one last bit of energy and offered his arm to his mother, escorting her to the bottom of the stairs. He kissed her cheek to say goodnight and turned away.

"You are not going to bed?" she asked.

"Not right away, I have some things to do." Daniel walked to his father's old study and closed himself inside. In vain did he try to shut out the beautiful memories of the evening that were dancing at his heels, begging to be acknowledged.

Begging to be remembered.

26

Were You Expecting Someone?

As if the heavens were fearful of Agnes Copeland's wrath, snow came the day following the Copeland Christmas ball. It covered Tree Town in white frosting, and the residents stayed in their homes, recovering from the late night of feasting and dancing.

The Tuesday following the dinner party, when Mrs. Bishop brought in the afternoon tea, Samantha didn't have the heart to tell her to take the extra teacup away. Daniel wouldn't be coming. She was sure of it, even though she hadn't received a note indicating otherwise.

She'd been proud of Daniel, during the ball. He'd performed splendidly. You'd never have known just a few days earlier, he'd had his heart broken. Still, while she'd seen a gradual change come over him the past few months, she predicted a return to the old sanctuary of sarcasm and cynicism in the face of discomfort.

Even with these predictions, she sorely hoped he'd

prove her wrong, though the old Daniel would likely fare better after tragedy than the one who had slowly come to care for the feelings of others.

William had already joined her when the bell rang. Samantha's heart leapt, then plummeted when she heard Rose's voice greeting Mrs. Bishop. The sister and her beau entered and warmed themselves by the hearth for a few minutes while they waited for Mrs. Bishop to bring another teacup.

"Were you expecting someone?" Rose glanced at the third cup already on the small table.

Samantha shook her head.

"Well, what did you think of the ball?" Rose took her seat. "It was far more enjoyable than anything I would have expected. I don't think I've ever been inside their home. Or if I have, I didn't recognize it. It was absolutely gorgeous. I wonder why they haven't had parties before."

"I was telling Rose I wouldn't have known Daniel Copeland from your descriptions of him," said Reuben. "He was very amiable and perfectly at ease."

"He surprised me as well," added Rose. "I wouldn't have recognized him either. Perhaps he's more comfortable in his own home?"

"Believe me, Daniel was far from comfortable," said Samantha, almost to herself. She sipped her tea and glanced at the clock on the mantle.

"It was kind of you to lead off the first dances. I thought for sure that role would fall to Victoria. But I barely saw them speak to one another. I can't make out that anything happened between them. She's been completely silent on the subject. Now, poor dear, she's come down with that cold that's been threatening for weeks."

"Is she all right?" asked William.

"Yes, yes. Dr. Vaughn has already seen her. He prescribed rest, and Mother has been plying her with ginger tea. If you ask me, she seems rather disheartened. I know something happened, but she didn't tell you anything, Samantha?"

Samantha shook her head, meaning to indicate she wouldn't reveal her sister's secret.

"Oh well," said Rose. "I suppose it's for the best. But unfortunate New Year's is too soon for an engagement for her. The challenge is lost just at the final hour."

They spoke on about the ball for a while. Samantha was pleased her family's general opinion of the evening was positive. Rose and Reuben even declared they'd return to Tree Town in future, if it became a regular part of the community's festivities.

After an hour or so, Mrs. Bishop came in with a fresh pot. As she was leaving, she hesitated at the door.

"Mrs. Bishop?" William inquired.

"I thought you ought to know, Mr. Copeland stopped by a bit ago. He heard you had company and said not to disturb you. He went away directly."

Samantha tensed, mortified at the unintended message he might have received.

"What could *he* want?" Rose asked.

"I thought for sure he wouldn't come today." Samantha's voice tightened with concern.

"Yes, there is quite a lot of snow outside."

Samantha found herself on the verge of tears.

Witnessing her distress, William patted her hand. "I'll go after him," he said.

"He's got to be nearly home by now."

"Then I'll head there immediately." William made his apologies to his friend and his sister-in-law and departed.

Rose looked confused. "Since when are you friendly with Daniel Copeland?"

"Since we asked him to begin taking tea with us every week. Over a month ago."

Reuben asked, "But isn't he—sort of—the enemy?"

"He's not the enemy. He's our friend."

Rose was aghast. "After he's done nothing but speak ill of our family? Wasn't that the whole point of the challenge in the first place?"

Samantha sat forward in her seat. "Yes, it was. But strangely, he's different these days. I think having true friends might have done him some good."

"He didn't seem that different a few weeks ago when Allison and I cautioned him to be careful with Victoria."

"You did?"

"He laughed at us. Seemed to think anything happening was absurd."

"Did you say anything about the challenge?"

"Of course not. He doesn't know that we know. But it *is* why we took the trouble of cautioning him. We knew he was just luring her away so she'd be too occupied to fall in love with someone."

"Yes, that was the idea."

"Do you suppose that's why they had a falling out?

Victoria discovered Daniel was only using her to win a bet?"

"You don't know they had a falling out," declared Samantha.

"We know something happened. If that boy broke her heart I'll never forgive him."

"Nor I," said Reuben.

Samantha sank deeper into her despair.

Alma Burros was sipping her tenth cup of tea that day. Cranky and pacing like a mother cat. She hated being cooped up indoors. The dreadful snow kept her from visiting the neighbors. After the dinner party she had so much to discuss with people. She wanted to talk about how Agnes Copeland had looked very regal, she'd hardly recognized her without her black silk. She wanted to discuss how Daniel Copeland has been such a charming host. Really, she hadn't ever seen him so friendly. When he'd opened the dances with Samantha Temple, it had caused a stir, as everyone knew he didn't like the Hartfords. He danced with *all* the Hartfords, and it was quite unexpected.

It *had* been reported he often visited the Temples — what was that about?

All of these things, Alma Burros was forced to ruminate over on her own, as she rocked back and forth in her parlor chair.

Suddenly, she paused her rocking. Were those voices she heard above the winter wind? Presently, she went to the window and saw two men outside her house speaking to one another. They were bundled up against the cold. Squinting to make out their dim figures, she jumped and nearly knocked her spectacles off her head when she realized it was Mr. William Temple and Mr. Daniel Copeland.

With hands shoved in pockets, shuffling back and forth to keep themselves warm, they conversed together. Whatever could they be speaking of in the middle of the road, surrounded by snow? She wanted desperately to make out the words. Alma pounded her fist on the windowsill. Perhaps she should invite them in. They were probably freezing. But then they would probably not talk about whatever it was they were talking about if they knew she was listening. How could she catch a drift of their conversation?

An idea formed. Desperately she tried to open the window, but it was stuck. She shook, wiggled, and banged to pry it loose. Finally it cracked free. The moment it was open, the freezing air outside began consuming the precious warm air inside. Triumphantly, she poked her head out the window, only to discover Mr. Copeland and Mr. Temple were gone. She pounded her fist on the windowsill again. They must have heard her. She reached up to close the window.

It was stuck.

27

Men, They Ruin Everything

For half a week, Daniel slowly composed a letter to Victoria. Determined to let her have her Christmas unimpeded by thoughts of him, he waited to send it until after the 25th of December.

Christmas with his mother was quiet, as it usually was. There was no physical evidence that a girl with untamable hair and green eyes had waltzed into their lives, disrupting it in the most pleasant way. The decorations for the party had been stored. Only the tree in the drawing room remained. The large rooms that had been opened to accommodate the guests were shut up once more, and the servants retreated out of sight.

But something had shifted for Daniel. Try as he might to resurrect his old habits of using his wit to tear down everything in range, the entertainment it once afforded had lost its appeal. Before, he always had something to say. Now—well—now he noticed the ornaments on the tree were the same ornaments his mother used every year. He turned one of the globes around, observing the intricate detail etched into the thin glass. He asked his mother where she had gotten the ornaments, and she informed him they were imported from France her first year in the house.

His mother gave considerable care to the smallest details in their home. He'd never paid attention before.

In the afternoon, he completed his letter. He'd re-written a few passages multiple times. He wasn't good at speaking his feelings, he certainly wasn't good at writing them. He only hoped to communicate how sorry he was and assuage her of any responsibility (should she be feeling any). Knowing his motives for securing her friendship had begun selfishly, he decided not to include that part. He'd come to genuinely care for her, so the root of it was unnecessary. Besides, revealing this would implicate Samantha and William, and there was no need for any rift to be formed in the family, however much he would have wished for it—just a few months ago.

William had come after him in the snow, the day he'd gone to visit and discovered they already had guests. It was just as well, he'd thought, as he turned away from the Temple's home and wandered through town. He'd been uncomfortable with the idea of seeing them after the party, afraid things in the friendship would have altered. It turned out, they hadn't been planning for him to come, so he'd left after telling the housekeeper (he still couldn't remember her name) not to disturb them.

Less than an hour later, William had caught up to him during his walk home.

They hadn't spoken since the party, and before that, they hadn't spoken of the events concerning Victoria. Old Daniel would have chosen to avoid the subject, but when William apologized for missing their engagement due to the unexpected visit of Rose and Reuben, Daniel took the opportunity to apologize for betraying William's trust after promising so faithfully to never hurt Victoria.

William was as gracious as Samantha, but admitted he'd been very angry and ready to end Daniel's life when first he heard of it. Daniel said he didn't blame him one bit. They shook hands and parted as friends, after Daniel agreed to visit every Tuesday before the date set for the Temple's move to the coast.

Daniel sealed the envelope containing Victoria's letter and left it on the writing desk in his father's study. He'd taken to using the study more these days. He'd spent most of his life determined not to think of his father, for fear the thinking would make him sad. He was right, of course, but he didn't mind the sadness now. He couldn't say he missed his father, as the memories of him were very sparse. He did, however, miss the idea of having a father.

He felt sure his father would have liked the Temples. And Victoria.

Christmas morning was always a lively affair at the Hartfords', but this year was especially lively. Reuben

Dudley was in town for the holiday. Samantha and William stayed the night Christmas Eve. Ethan and Aunt Letty walked over the minute the sun was up, and even Edward Cole had managed to come for breakfast, though he didn't stay long after that.

Laughter and cheerful spirits shook the house. At noon, Allison and Ethan began dividing teams for a snowman building contest, declaring it would be the first annual contest, and revealing a wooden plaque Ethan had carved as the prize for the winning team.

There was much good-natured banter, and only Samantha noticed when Victoria left the room.

She'd been quiet the whole morning, holed up on a couch with blankets wrapped around her and a cup of tea in her hands. She was still recovering from her cold, but Samantha suspected her spirits were affected by more than her waning illness.

After accepting her role on a team with Ethan and Rose, Samantha followed her youngest sister out into the hallway.

Victoria was seated on the stairs, head leaned wearily against the wall. She sighed when Samantha sank onto the step next to her. "Sorry, I didn't want to be a killjoy. You needn't stay. I can't go outdoors, anyway."

"What's wrong dear? You seem out of sorts."

Victoria took Samantha's hand. "I only wish that last Christmas I would have known it would be our last Christmas with just us. I don't mind that it's different, I just would have savored last year more, knowing everything would change forever."

"There are a lot of changes, aren't there? Usually

siblings get married gradually, but this year has been unusual."

"Last year, no one even talked about marriages or matches. Now our home is bursting with men, half of whom are strangers to me. I'm happy for you all. I just wish things hadn't changed quite so quickly."

Allison poked her head into the hallway. "Hey you, we're about to start," she called to Samantha.

"I'll be there in a moment."

Allison squinted, assessing the situation. She turned back to the parlor and beckoned to someone. Soon, the other three Hartford sisters were assailing the stairs.

"No sister meetings without us," said Rose.

"Move over Tori, you're hogging the best step," said Allison.

"Ouch! Ali, you stepped on my hand," cried Elizabeth.

"Sorry, just trying to cut down the competition."

They all squeezed together and enveloped Victoria in a human blanket. Within a few seconds she was laughing.

"That's better," said Allison. "What's this all about, anyway?"

"Too many changes all at once," Samantha answered.

"Ah, yes. It is a lot of change, isn't it?"

"I didn't realize until just now," said Rose. "With all these changes, each of us is getting something in return. But poor Victoria is only losing her sisters."

At this, Victoria's eyes welled up with tears and her nose began to run. Elizabeth handed her a handkerchief, but then had nothing to wipe her own eyes, so she used Allison's skirt.

"I don't want to bring down your joy," sniffed Victoria. "But I'm miserable."

They were all crying now.

"Men," said Allison. "They ruin everything."

"Men," agreed Elizabeth. "Nothing but a nuisance."

Ethan wandered into the hallway in search of his teammates. He stopped suddenly when he saw the sisters. Smiling apologetically, he retreated back into the parlor.

This caused a small trickle of laughter. The sisters wiped their eyes, and Allison declared Christmas night would be just sisters. No men.

Victoria collected all of her sisters' hands in hers. "You all are the dearest people in the world to me. Promise you won't forget about me?"

They all promised solemnly.

The snowman building contest was raucous and loud. Allison considered it her duty to sabotage the work of the others, and soon they were all building their snowmen in a battlefield of hurled snowballs.

It was well into the afternoon before the snowmen were complete and Victoria came outside to judge. She was bribed with all sorts of treats by the three teams until she finally declared Elizabeth, Mr. Hartford, and Reuben's team the winner. She nearly caught a snowball in the face from Allison, but William gallantly blocked it. Mrs. Hartford reprimanded Allison as she packed Victoria back into the house.

As Victoria rested inside for the remainder of the afternoon, she noticed the ache in her chest, which had arisen just before the Copeland ball, had decreased just a little.

While everything truly *was* different, she was content knowing her sisters were happy.

28

It is a Good Letter

Daniel dispatched his letter to Victoria first thing the day after Christmas. It was a warm day, considering the snow they'd been having, and he took Ebony out for a ride. He missed the presence of another set of hooves and knowing Victoria was close by. Sometimes they had spoken quite a lot while they rode, horse's neck and neck. Sometimes they hadn't spoken at all, and the ease with which they could talk, and not talk, had always been a comfort.

Once he'd returned to the stables, he gave Ebony a rubdown himself. The grooms worked near him and every once in a while glanced in his direction. He wondered what sort of conversations they had when he wasn't nearby.

Daniel had returned Ebony to his stall beside Angel and was putting the tack away when he got a familiar tingling sensation and turned around. His heart dropped into his stomach as Victoria entered the stables, her hair sprayed out beneath her hat, eyes alight with a fierce energy.

There was a shuffling sound behind him, and a glance over his shoulder revealed the grooms had made their escape.

Victoria held out a hand with his letter grasped between her fingers. "What is this?"

Daniel stared. Heart pounding.

"You seem to think loving me was some sort of crime."

Daniel swallowed. "Wasn't it?"

Victoria walked forward and sank into a seat on a barrel. "Why would you think that?" She gripped the letter in her lap.

Daniel fiddled with some riding tack, then he joined her on an adjacent barrel. "I made a mistake. I never should have kissed you. I never should have invited you here in the first place."

"But, *why*? I don't understand."

After some considerable silence—and some considerable thought—Daniel made a decision. He proceeded forward, knowing he might regret it. "There's one part of the story I didn't tell you in the letter. It's that, around eight months ago, I made a wager with Samantha and William. They had to have all the Hartford sisters engaged by the end of the year. So, that first time I met you and Elizabeth by the road, I concocted a plan to distract you both. Elizabeth, clearly, didn't take the bait. But you..." Daniel shifted so his body was facing hers. "You might have been the only person in town who was as lonely as I was. I took advantage of that. What's more, I promised Samantha and William I would never tamper with your heart. Though there was much I didn't understand, I knew full well the moment I came to care for you. I should have been more a master of my feelings. I was never a true friend to you, Victoria. And I am sorry."

There was another long silence as Victoria stared straight ahead. Finally, she spoke. "So all my sisters, their engagements were part of a game?"

"Your sister and brother were very careful. I can attest to it. They even cautioned Elizabeth against becoming engaged too soon. It started off as a game, but it all became very serious."

"And when you invited me to ride with you, you just wanted to keep me diverted? Did you never think of the possibility—with us spending so much time together—that something like this could happen?"

"I believed it improbable."

"Why?"

What went through Daniel's head sounded something like this: *you're Victoria, a beautiful, lively, and intelligent woman who speaks her mind and loves with her whole heart. I'm just Daniel. A cynical, bitter, and careless bumbler. It was the most improbable match anyone could think of.*

He also knew with certainty that the Hartfords would never accept him. It was more than certain. It was etched in stone. After the way he'd behaved, he deserved their censure forever.

And after he'd broken his promise to the only members of the family with whom he might have had a chance—no. There was no going back from that, even if they had forgiven him.

And just as certainly he knew, Victoria would never marry without her family's approval. He *knew*. He'd witnessed the matches of three sisters.

He didn't know how else to say it, so he repeated, "It's—improbable."

Victoria's green eyes glinted. "And what makes you so sure of this?"

Having no pride left, he said, "Because a Hartford would never love Daniel Copeland."

Victoria slumped a little, and a deep sadness overtook her features. Her mouth worked to try and say something, but no words came out.

With all the care and friendship of the past months, Daniel took hold of one of Victoria's hands. He stared at the hand as he said, "You deserve a good man. A kind man. Someone who will give you the world. One day, I'll watch you fall in love. And I won't mind, because I'll know then you are happy—that is all I could ever wish for."

Victoria looked about to withdraw her hand, but instead she squeezed his. "This is your objection? You are not good enough for me?"

"I know I am not."

"But what about what I think?"

Daniel stood. "Victoria, I hope and pray you can forget about how I've behaved. I hope you'll go on to live a long and happy life, and one day you'll not think on me at all. But, if you'll allow me to say this just once—know that I'll never forget about you."

A lone tear slid down Victoria's cheek. At the sight of it, Daniel clenched his fists. All he wanted to do was go to her, wrap her in his arms, and tell her how much he loved her. She was the best thing that had ever come into his life, and the short time they had together would be a memory laced in beauty and pain for the rest of his days.

Victoria rose from her seat.

"One more thing," Daniel said, as she turned to go. He indicated Ebony and Angel where they hung their heads over the stalls, affectionately nipping at one another. "Angel is yours. You can come fetch her anytime you like, or I'll have one of the grooms bring her over."

Victoria tilted her head. "But she is your horse."

Without lifting his eyes, Daniel said, "I bought her for you. I meant it as part of the distraction, but I always intended to give her to you."

Victoria glanced at the two horses. "They will not understand the separation. I think I'll leave her here, if you don't mind. And maybe, every once in a while, I can come ride?"

Daniel's heart somersaulted. Lacking coherency, he nodded.

"Goodbye, Daniel."

He managed to whisper, "goodbye" but she was already gone.

It was nearing afternoon tea when the doorbell rang. Samantha looked up, expecting to see one of her sisters, however she was shocked to see it was Victoria, pulling her scarf off and going to stand by the fireplace.

"Victoria! You're just recovering from a cold. You shouldn't be out in this weather yet."

"I needed to speak with you." She reached in her coat pocket and pulled out a letter. "Read this."

"What is it?" Samantha took the letter.

"It's a letter from Daniel."

"He wrote you a letter?"

"Yes. Go on, read it."

Samantha sat down and perused the letter. She read it three times without looking up. He apologized for his behavior, absolved Victoria of any responsibility, and thanked her for her kindness and forbearance. He said he knew the friendship was over, but hoped there was no permanent damage done. He'd left out some details of the story that she thought might cause Victoria some confusion, but all in all, he did the story justice, though perhaps Daniel was a bit too hard on himself. "It is a good letter," she said as she looked up.

"Is it?" Victoria said.

"Do not you think so?"

"No. And I told Daniel so just a few hours ago."

"You went to see him?"

Victoria was very calm, hands resting on her lap. "There is one problem with this whole debacle. Everyone was worried about Daniel's behavior toward me. You, William, and Daniel all seem to think it's unfortunate that he came to love me. But no one has once considered that I might love him."

Samantha remained still. "Are you saying—that you do love Daniel?"

"Yes."

Samantha's eyes grew wide.

"That he kissed me was unfortunate for the reasons that I stated. I felt if he'd had any chance of winning over my family, he ruined it. The timing could not have been worse, considering the ball and that I was supposed to be the hostess. But I never once said that the wrong lay with his regard for me.

"In truth, I believe I knew he was in love with me long before he ever did. I was quite aware I was falling in love with him, though I feared the disapproval of my family—no one but you and William seems to like him. Oh, and you should know, I know about the wager. Daniel informed me himself when I spoke with him today."

Samantha's eyes widened further. "He told you?"

"Yes. It helped fill in some of the gaps in the story—one of which was why Daniel invited me to ride with him, when it was widely known he disliked our family."

"He was using you."

"Yes, but no more than you were using my sisters."

Samantha conceded this was true. "Then you are not angry?"

"I am a little, but I'll recover. I have a feeling I'll find the whole thing very funny eventually. But for now, I need to know what you think of my being in love with Daniel."

"You are still in love with him?"

"Yes."

"And he, clearly, is still in love with you."

"Clearly."

Samantha shook her head, quite overcome. "I never imagined I'd ever say this, but it seems—probable."

"You are not disappointed?"

"No—oddly—though I am exceedingly surprised." Samantha inhaled. "It seems—as if—this is exactly the way this was supposed to end."

Victoria sat forward. "Then, Samantha, I am going to need your help with something."

29

A Stroke of Extreme Luck

The evening of December thirty-first, Daniel was reading by the fireplace. There was no better time to begin a resolution than the beginning of the New Year and he'd taken up the project of reading every book in his father's study, though he hadn't read a full book in years.

Nearing suppertime, his mother entered. She was wearing another dress with color. Violet and green. "Are you going somewhere?" he asked.

"To the New Year's celebration. But you are not dressed?"

Daniel gasped. "You never go to town functions."

Mrs. Copeland waved her hand. "I believe it my duty to attend this year, after everyone graced our home during our dinner party. I'm inclined to return the favor. But my boy, you are not staying home?"

"Yes, I believe I'll not attend this year."

"But you always go."

"I know. This year, I want to give Victoria a chance

to enjoy it without me around."

Mrs. Copeland grew sad. "You can't avoid her forever. This town is too small."

"I know. But it's her last New Year's with her sisters before they are all married. I'll not cast a shadow if I can avoid it."

Mrs. Copeland smiled warmly. "You've turned into a very thoughtful young man. I hope she will learn to appreciate it."

Daniel shook his head, but said nothing.

Mrs. Copeland surveyed her son. "You know, I never considered the Hartford girls worthy of you. Their family was working class, and I heard the rumors about their independence and impropriety. But, I think they may have changed my mind—about the land, that is."

"The land?"

"Your idea, to rent it out for profit. It is not a bad idea."

Daniel smiled. "I'll draw up a plan. We can discuss in the new year."

Mrs. Copeland nodded. "I'll be going now. I think you should come. I'm not a young woman anymore, and my bones tell me this will be a special night."

Daniel sat down and reopened his book. "Have a lovely time."

A few hours later, Daniel woke with a start. He'd fallen asleep, with the book on his chest. A servant must have rebuilt the fire, as it was blazing fiercely.

He'd had a thought in his dream that had jolted him awake. He'd been so consumed with giving Victoria the space she needed at the New Year's celebration that he'd forgotten a very important event that was supposed to occur at the party.

"Phillips!" he called. The butler came just a few moments later. "Have a groom saddle my horse. Quickly." It was nearing ten o'clock, and he just might make it in time.

He hadn't told Samantha and William not to announce their defeat. He hoped they'd have enough sense to forgo this part of the pact if he was not in attendance. But he couldn't be sure.

He fled upstairs to change.

Daniel, it seemed, had decided to skip the New Year's Eve party. Samantha craned her neck to look for him every time the door opened.

When Mrs. Copeland arrived without him, her heart sank. William, however, maintained hope. "I spoke to his mother and she seems to think he'll have a mind to come later."

Samantha drank more punch, and hoped his mother was right.

It was very close to midnight. "Should we make the announcement if he isn't here?" Samantha asked her husband.

Just then, William looked over the top of her head toward the door. He smiled. "Let's go," he said, leading her toward the stage.

The moment Samantha was standing center stage, every voice in the room became quiet and every eye in the room turned toward her. "You might have noticed quite a lot of Hartford sisters have become engaged this year." Laughter rippled throughout the room. "While no credit goes to any one person, it was not entirely a work of fate. For the past several months, Mr. Temple and I have been engaged in a pact with Daniel Copeland, winning only when all four of my sisters were engaged by the end of the year. Since that is not the case, it seems as if—"

"Hold up there!" A voice came from the back of the hall and Daniel rushed toward the stage. "You won after all. Part of the rules were, if you told anyone, you forfeit. I forfeit just a few days ago, when I told—someone—about the pact. Therefore, I concede willingly and the Hartfords will never again receive my condescension."

"Actually, you're still the winner." Allison had moved closer to the stage and stood up next to Samantha. Rose had made her way forward as well. "It turns out," said Allison. "That Rose and I discovered the pact by accident when we overheard you and Samantha speaking. We chose to abide by the original rules and not tell anyone outside of those who already knew, but, when Elizabeth became engaged, we decided she needed to know. So it was, in fact, us who forfeited."

"You knew?" Daniel's jaw dropped. "You all knew?"

Elizabeth had joined her sisters, and she smiled. "You see Daniel, you've won."

Someone spoke from the edge of the crowd—a crowd that parted when the speaker began to walk toward the stage. "It seems Daniel will be the loser after all." Daniel grew very still as he watched Victoria approach. "I happen to know, on this night, the final Hartford sister will be engaged before the stroke of midnight. What do you say to that?" Victoria planted herself several feet from Daniel.

In a voice clear and strong, Daniel said. "Whom is she marrying?"

Matching his clarity and strength, Victoria replied. "A good man. A kind man. Someone who makes her feel—whenever she is with him—that she could have the whole world."

Daniel lost all capacity to speak. He remained rooted to the floor as Victoria took a step closer. "She has decided, there is only one thing that would make her the happiest person among all her friends and family, and that would be for him to say yes to a proposal of marriage. But he has a little time to think on it. The youngest Hartford sister awaits his answer."

Daniel glanced around at the other sisters who, at that moment, flanked him. "But what about your family?" he asked.

"You dunderhead," said Allison. "Of course we approve."

"We wouldn't be standing here if we didn't," said Rose.

A nervous chuckle from the crowd enveloped them as Daniel lifted his eyes to meet Victoria's. She was too far away for him to reach out and pull her near, and he felt if he took one step, he might collapse. He continued staring into her shining green eyes as his heart and soul swelled so they seemed to consume one another.

"Well," Victoria said, voice barely above a whisper.

"What might be his reply?"

Slowly, Daniel held out a hand. His grin stretched into a smile that stretched across his entire face. The crowd pressed in, shoving Victoria into Daniel's arms. He lent down and pressed his cheek against hers, his own moist with tranquil tears. "He says yes. Yes, my love, yes."

It wasn't midnight yet, but someone began singing Auld Lang Syne. Glasses were raised, and the Hartford family enfolded Daniel and Victoria with hugs and kisses and cheers of happiness.

As the celebration carried on, Victoria told Daniel how it all came about. After she left him at the stables, she'd gone to Samantha's to tell her about the letter. She'd told Samantha that while everyone was aware Daniel was in love with her, no one had imagined she might have fallen in love with him.

With Samantha and William's help, Victoria called together her entire family (including the new beaus) and told them the whole story. Elizabeth, it turned out, had already heard about the pact from Rose and Allison. Only Mr. and Mrs. Hartford were surprised, and Mr. Hartford asked to speak to each of his daughters privately, to ensure they were not marrying under duress (though the happy faces in the room confirmed this was not the case).

Victoria then informed them of her plan, as she knew Daniel would need something very drastic to convince him she loved him just as much as he loved her.

The plan was almost foiled when Daniel didn't show for the New Year's celebration.

Daniel filled in this detail as to how he'd wanted to give Victoria a chance to enjoy her family without his presence, but then he remembered the addition of the admittal of defeat to the original pact and had come in hopes of stopping William and Samantha, should they attempt to go through with it.

These declarations did the trick to endear Daniel to the Hartford family, who had already chosen to love him for Victoria's sake.

Some said the Hartford sisters would never marry. Those same people who witnessed the Hartford family miracle, whispered behind their hands that it was a very strange year indeed.

Many months later, Daniel would remark to Samantha, "Irony of ironies, if I'd just waited, Victoria would never have become engaged. I would have won the challenge, and Victoria and I would have never fallen in love."

"You know," said Samantha. "All of this proves you were right. William and I did have a stroke of extreme luck. While we all took part, there was so much out of our control. We sincerely were lucky. All of us."

"Yes, all us. I most of all."

The End

Epilogue

Daniel's Speech on Rose's Wedding Day

I remember the day Reuben Dudley departed Tree Town after his first brief visit. I think the whole town suspected Samantha and William had brought him here to form a match between him and one of the sisters. I, however, *knew* that was their intention, so great was my relief when he left and there were no wedding bells.

Imagine my surprise when I heard, just a few months later, he and Rose were in engaged. I was terribly angry, because it meant I was just that much closer to losing a bet. I was also appalled, as I believed—along with most of the town—the Hartford sisters would never marry.

When fate had other plans, it caused me to wonder how marriage became a sign and seal of some mystical status, and only those who are unworthy never attain it.

I believe the Hartfords answered this question years before any of us. It was the reason for their happiness when the rest of us considered them quite strange. So the reality Reuben Dudley was able to see past what the rest of us could not, in just a few short months, speaks to a depth of character worthy of a kind and endearing woman.

To Mr. and Mrs. Rueben Dudley, may you both continue to see beyond what the rest of us cannot, and may your life be as colorful and glorious as Rose's creations.

Allison's Wedding Day

Okay, okay. I'll make this brief as I don't want to steal the spotlight from the happy couple.

Allison: oh, we don't mind. (Satisfied smile)

Ethan: yes, please, take all the time you like. (Enjoying watching Daniel pay his dues)

Growing up around Allison and Ethan wasn't easy. They were both very competitive, always challenging each other and keeping everyone around them on their toes. You never knew what they were going to do next. *(Understanding murmur from the crowd)*

Then one day, out of nowhere, they were engaged. But I've heard the story (as I'm sure all of you have) and it seems the match was sealed in heaven long ago, as neither of them had eyes for anyone else.

It takes great fortitude to love someone your whole life. Especially during the span of a lengthy separation. I am confident this fortitude will see them through anything that comes their way. Not only are they a match built on love. They are a match built on friendship. Let us toast to love and friendship, as there is nothing better than being in love with someone you consider your best friend. May you both challenge one another until you reach a ripe old age, and may your love grow stronger each and every day.

(Allison and Nathan both pretend to have something in their eye)

Elizabeth's Wedding Day

I have Elizabeth to thank for one very important part of my own love story. Once, when I thought to distract both sisters from marriage, Elizabeth didn't take the bait. I wonder now what would have happened if she'd not been distracted by her own match, if Elizabeth and Edward Cole had not fallen for one another when they did.

As it happens, I cannot imagine two people more suited for one another. Your strength of character and willingness to sacrifice for the ones you love is an example to us all. Your goodness will always bring happiness wherever you go, and anyone who knows you is the better for it.

You have both spent so much of your lives serving those around you. I know no one more deserving of happiness, and I wish it in abundance upon both of you.

Victoria's Wedding Day

But first, before I begin, I'll conceded my wife is far better at speeches than I am. And I would like to think, had there not been a wager to win, I would be making this speech anyway. You see, it's difficult to find ways to express in words how I feel, especially when I made a habit of finding the base and unattractive everywhere I looked.

That was until you entered my life. I couldn't understand why you were so damned happy—excuse me—but you were. You found joy in everything. You might have been a species from another world, how foreign your contentment was to me.

Then we spent more time together and I saw beneath the joy a depth of intelligence with which I could not compete, so imagine my devastation when I realized I was falling in love.

Yes, there was a bet to win. Yes, I'd spent most of my life disliking your family and making sure everyone knew how much.

But the greatest part of my distress was the realization, at the same time as my discovery of being in love, that you were far too good for me, far above me in every possible way. There was no world in which I could ever think to earn your love.

So the fact I'm standing here today, I know the greatest miracle of this past year is *not* that all five Hartford sisters are married. The greatest miracle is that I am your husband and you are my wife and I get to spend the rest of my life marveling at how wonderful it feels to love you and be loved by you.

To Victoria Hartford Copeland—the best decision I ever made was trying to keep you from getting married.

About the Author

Katherine Spearing was a teenager when she wrote the first version of *Hartfords*, sitting on her bed surrounded by her real-life sisters. With a Bachelor of Arts in English and a Master of Arts in Religion and Cultures, you will find her writing during the dark hours of the day and running a nonprofit the rest of the time. She hosts the *Uncertain* podcast and writes regularly at katherinespearing.com. Follow her on Instagram: @katherinespearing

Subscribe!

Subscribe to the mailing list and receive monthly updates from the author and opportunities to win free stuff!

CPSIA information can be obtained
at www.ICGtesting.com
Printed in the USA
BVHW031539180921
616989BV00005B/15

9 781736 711903